PUFFIN

HOW TO BE A SUPER SPY

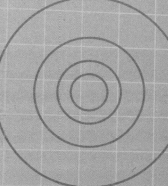

E. YOUNG

PUFFIN BOOKS

Published by the Penguin Group

Penguin Books Ltd, 80 Strand, London WC2R ORL, England

Penguin Group (USA) Inc., 375 Hudson Street, New York, New York 10014, USA

Penguin Group (Canada), 90 Eglinton Avenue East, Suite 700, Toronto, Ontario,
Canada M4P 2Y3 (a division of Pearson Penguin Canada Inc.)

Penguin Ireland, 25 St Stephen's Green, Dublin 2, Ireland (a division of Penguin Books Ltd)

Penguin Group (Australia), 250 Camberwell Road, Camberwell, Victoria 3124,
Australia (a division of Pearson Australia Group Pty Ltd)

Penguin Books India Pvt Ltd, 11 Community Centre, Panchsheel Park,
New Delhi – 110 017, India

Penguin Group (NZ), cnr Airborne and Rosedale Roads, Albany, Auckland 1310,
New Zealand (a division of Pearson New Zealand Ltd)

Penguin Books (South Africa) (Pty) Ltd, 24 Sturdee Avenue, Rosebank, Johannesburg
2196, South Africa

Penguin Books Ltd, Registered Offices: 80 Strand, London WC2R ORL, England

www.penguin.com

First published 2005

5

Text copyright © Emma Young, 2005
Design and illustrations copyright © John Fordham, 2005
All rights reserved

The moral right of the author and illustrator has been asserted

Made and printed in England by Clays Ltd, St Ives plc

British Library Cataloguing in Publication Data

A CIP catalogue record for this book is available from the British Library

ISBN 0-141-31789-2

CONTENTS

		1
INTRODUCTION		3
CHAPTER 1	PREPARE FOR ACTION	22
CHAPTER 2	SPY TALK	46
CHAPTER 3	THE ART OF SURVEILLANCE	61
CHAPTER 4	DISTANCE IS NO OBJECT	78
CHAPTER 5	MIND CONTROL	92
CHAPTER 6	ESSENTIAL KIT	105
CHAPTER 7	MOVE IT!	122
CHAPTER 8	NEED TO KNOW	132
CHAPTER 9	THE ACTION	

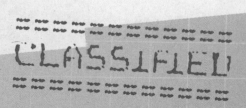

CLASSIFIED

INTRODUCTION

TO BE A TOP MODERN SPY
YOU'LL NEED TO KNOW
MORE THAN INTERNATIONAL
FLIGHT TIMETABLES.

You'll have to work hard at becoming
an expert in psychology, technology,
self-defence and communications.

You'll know all about high-tech transport.

You'll be able to encrypt a message and decode a text. You'll be a whizz at spotting a liar at fifty paces, trailing someone without them suspecting, and calling your boss with a phone hidden inside your tooth . . .

HOW WILL YOU DO IT?

Your first step is to locate your spy training manual. Within it, you'll find all you need to survive – and thrive.

WHERE CAN YOU FIND IT?

That's easy. It's in your hands!

Now all *you* need to do is read on.

Sir Stephen, retired British spymaster, and investigative journalist Spencer Bing will help you on your way.

CHAPTER 1
PREPARE FOR ACTION

LOCATION: YOUR BEDROOM

TIME: TO PREPARE FOR LIFE AS A SPY

There's one fact you'll have to take on board now: intelligence organizations only recruit adults. So you'll have to wait a little while before you can start work. But in the meantime, you'll need to do two things:

- **learn now about how to become a top spy**
- **practise real spy techniques**

This book contains all the information you'll need.

You already know this: you want action and thrills and adventure.

But first, there are some very important questions to consider.

Do you know *exactly* what type of spy you want to be?
Who do you want to work for?
How will you actually get your job?

In fact, the process of becoming a spy is almost as exciting as the spying itself!

Study the files that follow closely. You'll need to know their contents in detail:

TOP SECRET: / RECRUITMENT FILE #1

NAME: The Secret Intelligence Service - SIS
      (Also Known As - AKA - MI6)
AKA: 'The Firm' to members, 'The Friends' to
      other spy agencies
MISSION: To gather 'intelligence' outside the
      UK (In other words, to snoop overseas)

ESTABLISHED: 1912

HEADQUARTERS: South London, England, with
    stations around the world
MAILING ADDRESS: 85 Albert Embankment,
    Vauxhall Cross,
    London SE1
WEB ADDRESS: None
NUMBER OF EMPLOYEES:
    Secret

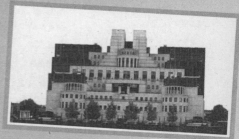

FAST FACT: The first chief of SIS was Sir
    Mansfield Smith Cumming, who signed
    himself 'C'. According to tradition, all SIS
    chiefs are known by the same single letter

And if you want to get a top posting with the SIS, this is *the*
'C' you'll really have to impress:

SPY SUPREMO

Name: JOHN SCARLETT
Joined SIS: 1970
Occupation: Chief of the
Secret Intelligence Service, MI6

Scarlett worked as an intelligence

officer in SIS offices in Nairobi, Moscow and Paris before becoming head of the SIS station in Moscow. In 2001, he became chairman of the Cabinet Office Joint Intelligence Committee — a committee that includes all the chiefs of all Britain's intelligence agencies. He was then made chief of the SIS in May 2004.

Scarlett has a first class degree in history from Oxford University and speaks fluent Russian. He lists his interests as history, medieval churches and family.

TOP SECRET:

RECRUITMENT FILE #2

NAME: The Central Intelligence Agency (the CIA)

AKA: 'The Company'

MISSION: Like the SIS, to gather intelligence abroad. Officially:

• To provide accurate and timely intelligence on foreign threats to US security

- To conduct counter-intelligence activities or other special activities relating to foreign intelligence and national security, when the President asks us to

ESTABLISHED:
1947

HEADQUARTERS:
  Langley, Virginia, United States, also with stations around the world
MAILING ADDRESS: Central Intelligence Agency, Office of Public Affairs, Washington, D.C. 20505, USA
WEB ADDRESS: www.cia.gov
NUMBER OF EMPLOYEES: Secret

FAST FACT: There's one CIA group you'll never be able to join. In fact, to be a member of the K-9 Corps, you have to be a dog. This corps of dogs, trained to sniff out tiny amounts of explosive, was set up in 1991

And to get on within the CIA, this is the guy to thrill with your raw spy skills:

SPY SUPREMO

Name: PORTER GOSS
Joined CIA: 1960
Occupation: Director
of the Central Intelligence
Agency (CIA)

Goss was recruited by the CIA during
his junior year at Yale University.
He joined Army Intelligence in 1960
before working for the CIA's most
well-known division, the Directorate
of Operations. Goss served in Congress
for sixteen years and was House
Intelligence Chairman for eight of
those years.

Goss graduated from Yale with a Bachelor
of Arts degree in Classics and Greek.
He also speaks Spanish and Russian.

OK, now you know the agency facts.

But how will you get yourself recruited?

Ever seen an ad like this?

WANTED

Clever young people to safeguard our future.

MUST BE WILLING TO:
• Drive fast cars • Fire weapons
• Work in disguise • Abseil down mountains
• Interrogate evil masterminds

Of course not.

If you want to work as a British spy overseas, you'll need to get a job with the SIS. But the SIS doesn't advertise – at least not so obviously. To spot a real ad for a spy, you'll need an eagle eye, and a good idea of what you're looking for. Here's how a real SIS advert might read:

Are you a success in your chosen career?
But are you bored?
Looking for something more demanding –
even dangerous? If you're over eighteen and a high-level achiever, write to us.
We just might have the job for you . . .

(Note: As the job description will never clearly state 'spy', you'll just have to try your luck with an advert like this, and hope the job isn't for a lion tamer!)

If you have American citizenship, then you can apply to join the CIA. To learn more about the types of job on offer, let's take a peek at the notes of Spencer Bing (real name: Jack Smith), ambitious young journalist on a spy industry newspaper called *The Insider* ...

Headed State-side to check out the Yankee competition. Waited outside CIA HQ and followed a likely looking gent with a briefcase and a sharp suit.
INTENTION: Follow and learn
REALITY: He walked to the car park, got in a car and drove off
RESULT: I lost him
CONCLUSION: Bad day. Must do better

Next morning, woke up, decided to use my top investigative skills to get to the truth.
(TRANSLATION: I picked up the phone and dialled the press office ...) Here's what they told me:

The CIA has four different major departments:

1. DIRECTORATE OF OPERATIONS
EMPLOYS: 'Case officers'. People who like to travel overseas, speak different languages, be brave and keep secrets
TRANSLATION: Action spies

2. DIRECTORATE OF SCIENCE AND TECHNOLOGY
EMPLOYS: People who are brilliant at science and engineering
TRANSLATION: Gadget-making super-stars

3. DIRECTORATE OF INTELLIGENCE
EMPLOYS: People who can sort through mounds of information and make sense of it all
TRANSLATION: Geniuses of analysis

4. MISSION SUPPORT OFFICES
Five offices that employ doctors, financial whizzes, training experts, etc.
TRANSLATION: People who support spies

If you want to join the CIA, here's what you could do:

1. Write a letter and ask to be a 'clandestine operative' (a spy).
   Chance of getting a job: Minute

2. Answer a job ad for an intelligence officer (a spy).
   Chance of getting a job: Minute–medium

3. Wait for the CIA to approach you.
   Chance of getting a job: Not bad

And if you are lucky enough to be invited to take part in the interview process, this is what will happen ...

You'll be invited to Washington for several days of grilling.

During this time you'll:

- **Take an IQ test. Cheat and you'll be out of there!**
- **Have your personality assessed by psychologists**
- **Be examined in real spy-style scenarios**
- **Take a lie-detector test**
- **Have a thorough medical examination**

If you're brilliant enough to make it through, CIA investigators will spend anything from weeks to months checking you out. They'll visit your home town, your university, and they might even visit your old school! All this to make sure you really are who you claim to be.

If you pass all those tests AND you're telling the truth, you're in. At least, you're a Career Trainee.

Now the hard work really starts!

All spy trainees – whether with the CIA or the SIS – are sent to specialist facilities for intensive instruction.

If you're with the SIS, you'll go to Fort Monckton, a Napoleonic fort in Hampshire.

If you're with the CIA, you'll go to Camp Peary in Virginia, aka 'The Farm'. And to Fort Bragg, North Carolina – for heavy-weapons training with the special forces.

TRAINING FILE

NAME: Fort Monckton

DESCRIPTION: Built in the 1780s, the fort was updated in the 1860s, and used as a barracks for the Royal Engineers. The only way in is across a drawbridge and through a portcullis INSIDE: an indoor pistol range, a gym, labs and lecture rooms OUTSIDE: a helicopter landing pad

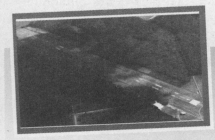

TRAINING FILE

NAME: Camp Peary

DESCRIPTION: Country club, with tennis courts, swimming pool, fishing boats for the river. Recruits live in dormitories; instructors in houses on site

The training regime is tough. This is a typical day's timetable for a spy recruit:

07.00: Martial arts training
08.30: Theory of desert survival
10.00: Explosives!
11.30: Circuit training
12.00: Secret photography

```
13.00:  Lunch (you'll have to find what
        you can from the grounds)
14.00:  Activity: Blindfolded and driven
        in van for two hours. Dumped in
        middle  of  countryside.  Wallet
        emptied. Ordered to race other
        trainees back to base
```

But that's not all. As a rookie spy ...

- You'll be put in **dangerous situations**. Instructors will try to punch you. 'Hostage-takers' will fire blanks at you
- You'll be ordered to **abseil** down through a roof
- You'll be told to scale a wall, and drive a car brilliantly – at **top speed**
- You'll learn **how to lie** and how to spot other brilliant liars
- You'll be able to walk into a room full of people and **check them out** without anyone noticing. Later, you'll be able to describe in detail how they looked and what they were wearing
- You'll learn how to listen to three conversations in three different languages – **all at the same time**
- You'll learn how to greet ambassadors, and how to **steal their secrets**
- You'll be trained in the very latest **secret gadgetry** for communications and surveillance
- You'll learn how to persuade people to turn against their own country and hand **vital information** to you

Sounds tough? Well, don't panic: you'll learn all you need to know about these skills in the following chapters. The book you're holding right now is a training manual for all would-be spies.

If you do make it with the SIS or the CIA, you'll be assigned either to the secret spying service, or to one of the offices that supports spies.

If you make it as an outdoor-action kind of spy, you'll take one of two roles:

• An 'official cover' spy

You might be assigned to be a minor 'diplomat' in an embassy overseas. But this job title is a cover – just an excuse for you to be in the country. Rather than (or sometimes as well as) doing diplomatic work, you'll be engaged in outdoor action-spying at its best

• A 'non-official cover' spy

You'll work deep undercover and alone. You'll have to think extra-fast on your feet if you're to stay alive. A non-official cover spy might be someone working as an archaeologist or a personnel officer in a big oil firm – they have 'real jobs', and only they and their contacts back at their intelligence base know their true mission. When you're not being a 'regular' worker in a 'regular' office, you'll be spending all your time gathering intelligence and secretly sending it back to your HQ. Like official cover spies, you'll be in the thick of the action. One morning, you could be inspecting an archaeological site. That afternoon, you could be on the road, heading for a meeting with an anxious agent at a 'closed' holiday resort ...

Part of working undercover means taking on another identity. Not only will you get a new name, with a passport, bank statements and other ID to match, you'll have a made-up family and life history that you'll share with anyone who asks. Learning all this new history will take some time. But if you've ever wanted to change your name or pretend to be somebody else – now's your chance.

Why not have a go now at making up your own new identity? And why not ask a few of your friends to do the same? Give yourselves new names and hobbies, and new families. Then try to act out your identities for one whole day.
Tip: Don't choose a school day – your teachers might not understand!

Now you know about 'official' and 'non-official' cover, let's clear up some more spy terminology.

'Agents' are the people that SIS or CIA officers recruit to find out secrets or pass on information to them. The officer then acts on that intelligence or sends it back to their base, so someone else can help them make sense of it. Agents are usually foreigners.

The path of information flow and control runs like this:

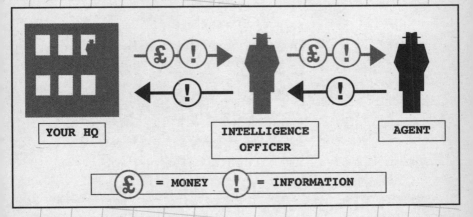

YOUR HQ   INTELLIGENCE
                          OFFICER   AGENT

£ = MONEY   ! = INFORMATION

If you were an **intelligence officer** working in a foreign country **undercover** as an embassy diplomat, you might recruit the chauffeur of a local government minister as an **agent**. Your chauffeur-agent could then give you juicy details about his boss's plans – probably in return for wads of cash.

Once you've got the details from your agent, you'll write up your info and send it back to SIS HQ. Depending on how important that report is, you'll give it a rating of one to five stars. A five-star report goes straight to top members of the government.

So, now you know how to become an **overseas operative**. But there are other spying organizations with a focus closer to home. While the SIS concentrates on foreign activities, MI5 focuses on threats to Britain. If you think you might enjoy action in the UK, read on.

RECRUITMENT FILE # 3

NAME: The Security Service (MI5)

MISSION: The UK's security intelligence agency. Officially: 'We are responsible for security intelligence work against covertly organized threats to the nation. These include terrorism, espionage and the proliferation of weapons of mass destruction'

ESTABLISHED: 1916

LOCATION: Thames House, Millbank, London

MAILING ADDRESS: The Enquiries Desk, PO Box 3255, London SW1P 1AE

WEB ADDRESS: www.mi5.gov.uk

NUMBER OF EMPLOYEES: About 3000

The boss of MI5 is female.

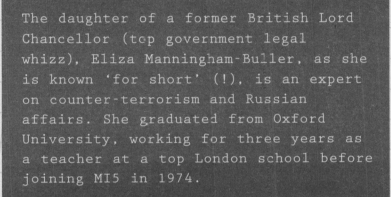

SPY SUPREMO

Name: ELIZABETH LYDIA
MANNINGHAM-BULLER
Born: 1948
Occupation: Director General of MI5

The daughter of a former British Lord
Chancellor (top government legal
whizz), Eliza Manningham-Buller, as she
is known 'for short' (!), is an expert
on counter-terrorism and Russian
affairs. She graduated from Oxford
University, working for three years as
a teacher at a top London school before
joining MI5 in 1974.

As you can see from the training file, MI5 has a website where you can read all about current vacancies. You can apply to be anything from a driver to a surveillance officer.

Trainee surveillance officers spend at least two months under intense instruction – then, if they pass, they're qualified to join the Mobile Surveillance Unit. (Note: you'll learn all about surveillance in the next few chapters.)

Trainee 'generalists' – intelligence officers (analysts and action spies!) – spend at least six months learning the ropes.

Then there are further training courses and specialist programmes to build your skills.

MI5, the SIS and the CIA all want action spies who will blend in with the crowd. Men who are taller than 5 feet 11 inches, and women who are taller than 5 feet 8 inches (coincidentally, just about the same height as Eliza Manningham-Buller herself!) might find it difficult to get clearance for secret MI5 work in the field. But instead they can find a home at MI5 HQ . . .

Here's what MI5 has to say about its own headquarters: 'It is air-conditioned with up-to-date workstations and office automation systems. It contains good facilities for staff including a restaurant, shop, multi-gym and squash courts.'

So if the idea of serving your country doesn't appeal to you, perhaps you'll be swayed by the facilities!

As with would-be CIA or SIS spies, everyone who applies to join MI5 will be thoroughly checked out. You'll have to fill in detailed questionnaires about your life and experience. An officer will then go through your answers in detail, and track down all kinds of people who know you, to make sure that you're telling the truth and to find out more about you.

Tip: Now might be the time to start being nice to your maths teacher – one day you just might need a good word from him or her.

Got all that?

Good. You're fully briefed on the background.
Now, it's time *to learn about action* . . .

CHAPTER 2
SPY TALK

LOCATION: THE FIELD

COLLEAGUES IN THE
FIELD: WILL AND DAMIAN

TIME: JUST AFTER DAWN

Imagine this: You're on a top-secret mission in remote south-east Asia. Just a few metres away is a semi-concealed military base. The light's still dim, and it's hard to make out your surroundings with the naked eye. Using your night-vision binoculars you spot Damian and Will in position behind a clump of trees beyond the base. Then you watch an army officer in full military kit stride from the base towards a weapons silo. You recognize him instantly from the files: General Pedro, the crazy arms dealer, no doubt about it. Behind Pedro, another man. He turns his face towards you. You blink. Can it be . . .? No . . . Is it really Richard 'Rudy' Rawcus, your old spy-training buddy – a key officer with the SIS? And now – surely not – *a double-dealing bad guy*?

You need to inform Will and Damian and HQ – fast. But how? Even the best information can be useless unless you can pass it on securely. To be a top spy, you'll need to know all about **secret communications**.

CONVERSATION KIT

To get the word out on Rudy, you could use a mini earpiece and microphone set-up to talk to Damian and Will, and you might use a mobile phone to inform HQ.

The earpiece will fit right inside your ear, and you will have attached the microphone to your clothing or even your body. This system will keep you in constant voice contact with your two colleagues.

But what if you managed to sneak up very close to General Pedro and Rudy? You've managed to whisper the truth to Will, with no one overhearing you. But the last thing you want is the sound of his voice, calling back in loud disbelief!

TALKING TEETH

Instead of the standard earpiece, one option might be to use the **tooth phone**.

This really is a phone that fits right in a tooth. (You'd have to have one hollowed out for the purpose!) At the moment, the British designers have created only a prototype – a basic working model – of the system. It has two components:

1. A digital radio receiver: This receiver takes incoming radio signals (carrying Will's voice) and turns them into quiet sound.

2. A vibrating component: This component transmits the sound to your ear by vibrating the bones in your jaw and ear! So you could listen to Will's exclamations – but General Pedro and Rudy wouldn't have a hope of hearing a thing.

Or, you might even be able to use . . .

SILENT SPEECH

NASA, the American space agency, is working on 'secret' talking devices. They've developed a computer program that takes input from sensors placed under your chin and on each side of your 'larynx'– or voice box. The larynx is part way down your neck, at the front. (When boys reach puberty, the larynx grows larger and sticks right out in a lump – then, it's often known as an Adam's apple.)

NASA says this system can pick up signals sent from your brain to your speech organs when you think about words. These signals could then be transmitted to Will, for example, without anyone close by being able to overhear. In other words, you can send your thoughts to others without speaking.

Of course, telling HQ and Will about Rudy is all very well – but ideally you want your voice signal to be secret, so that an enemy agent tapping into your conversation won't be able to understand the meaning of your words. To do this, you'll need a cipher or code.

CIPHER

A system for replacing letters or numbers, according to a rule or **key**.

Aim: To conceal your meaning from any outsider.

A very simple cipher key could run like this: *'Replace each letter with the next in the alphabet.'*

So **RUDY** would become **SVEZ**.

To *de-cipher* 'SVEZ' the person receiving the message would have to know the key (or be able to work it out).

You might hear spies talk about the **encryption** and **decryption** of messages. Encryption means taking a message and making it secret using a cipher key. Decryption means using the cipher key to reveal the original message.

CODE

A system for replacing words or phrases with other words and phrases, to conceal the meaning.

Just as James Bond was given the codename 007, Rudy, as a member of the SIS, would also have had a codename. Let's say it was BLUE DOG.

And let's say, according to your agreed code with HQ, a traitor is known as a TWO-SCOOP.

You could grab a standard mobile phone from your pocket, dial HQ and say: 'Blue dog's a two-scoop' and – hopefully – only you and the person at the other end would have a clue what you were talking about!

 You could use a code with your friends at school, or with your brothers or sisters.
If you decided that:

BROCCOLI = CLOUD
DISGUSTING = CARROT

You could shout, 'This cloud is carrot!' at teatime, and your mum wouldn't have a clue ...

Warning: *Make sure you explain that you're using a code or she could call the doctor ...*

MATHS MAGIC

Of course, anyone overhearing your coded message about Rudy wouldn't understand what you were on about. But how could you use a cipher to report the truth? Surely it would take too long to translate what you want to say into an encrypted message?

In fact, you can use 'secure' mobile phones that do the encrypting and decrypting automatically.

Using complex maths, the system will scramble the transmission of your words thoroughly, and unscramble them at the other end. For example:

YOU: *'Rudy's a traitor!'* – scrambled

HQ: unscrambled. *'I don't believe it!'* – scrambled

YOU: unscrambled. *'He's here with Pedro!'* – scrambled

will seem like a normal conversation.

Some people employed by secret services dedicate their time to coming up with clever codes and ciphers – and to cracking those for which they don't know the key. The people who crack them are called cryptologists (cryp-tol-ogists) or sometimes 'cryptanalysts'. Often, they're brilliant mathematicians who can see patterns in letters or numbers that normal people just can't spot. But modern cryptologists don't use only their minds to crack codes and ciphers – they also use massive amounts of computer power.

In fact, the very first computers resulted from machines developed for just that purpose: to crack encrypted messages and so to save British lives in the Second World War. Let's find out more from the memoirs of Sir Stephen (surname withheld to protect his identity), retired top SIS spy . . .

The Memoirs of Sir Stephen
CHAPTER 941: BLETCHLEY PARK

Ah, the glorious past of cryptography. Daring young folks, making symbols, saving lives. And never more true than at old Bletchley. Bletchley Park, that is, in southern England. Stately home and secret hotspot during those difficult war years.

The problem, you see, was the German Enigma cipher machine. Tough as my old mother, I like to say . . . And it took a tough-minded set of mathematical magicians to break it.

What was the Enigma machine? Well, it looked a bit like a big old-fashioned typewriter. But as you typed your message, electrical impulses sent through a series of wheels and wires created encrypted text. This text read as gobbledygook.

To make it even more difficult to crack, German operators transmitted daily instructions on how to change the set-up of the Enigma machine. This meant that the 'key' you needed to read the text was completely different each day.

This machine could encrypt a message in 150 million million million different ways! Fiendishly brilliant stuff!

Were we daunted? Well, yes. Were we beaten? Of course not!

Working in cold, damp huts around Bletchley Park, British mathematical geniuses (with the help of key info from Polish experts and British intelligence officers – not least, I am compelled to admit, myself) solved the problem. Maths virtuoso Alan Turing created a machine called the Bombe, which massively sped up the process of breaking the Enigma key every day – and the system was cracked. (In fact, this Bombe marked a huge step towards modern computers. But that, my dear readers, is another story . . .)

Think you'd be good at cracking tough ciphers?

Then have a go at these 'easy' examples. Write out the alphabet on a piece of paper if you need to – it might help.

1. ROHDR ZQD RMDZJX
Clue: 'Dog' would become 'cnf'

2. OGGV OG VQPKIJV
Clue: 'Boy' would become 'dqa'

3. ENOD LLEW
Clue: Think backwards

Answers:

1. **'SPIES ARE SNEAKY'** The key to creating the cipher text is: *'Use the letter that is one to the left in the alphabet.'*
2. **'MEET ME TONIGHT'** The key to creating the cipher text is: *'Use the letter that is two to the right in the alphabet.'*
3. **'WELL DONE'** The key to creating the cipher text is: *'Reverse the letters in the message.'*

 Have a go at coming up with your own cipher keys or codes. What about:

• Replace each letter with the number of its position in the alphabet (so A=1, D=4, Z=26, and so on)

• Replace the first part of the alphabet with a phrase:

ABCDEFGHIJKLMNOPQRSTUVWXYZ

would become

IMASPYBCDEFGHJKL NOQRTUVWXZ

And you'd use this cipher alphabet instead. So to send the message: 'SEE YOU AT DAWN', you'd write 'QPP XKT IR SIVJ'.

SIR STEPHEN'S TOP CRYPTO-TIPS:

If you're trying to decrypt a long bit of text, and you suspect the cipher involves replacing one letter with one other, here are some hints for working it all out . . .

- EE and OO are common letter pairs. So if you see a few TTs in that text, the T could stand for an E or an O

- A, E, I, O or U are in almost every word – if you can work out the vowels, you're doing well

- The most common three-letter word is THE. Find a few identical three-letter groups in the text, and you might just have found the letters standing for T, H and E!

Breaking ciphers can be very tricky, of course. Especially because the rule about making cipher keys is: as long as they're logical, there are none! You can make them as difficult as you like!

Note: Ciphers don't always rely on one 'cipher' letter corresponding to one meaningful letter.

 Can you find the secret note in this apparently 'normal' answerphone message?

'Really good day on the slopes. Until I catapulted off my snowboard. Damaged my bum! Yeah, it really hurt. I had to see the doctor. Said it wasn't my fault. But he wasn't very sympathetic. Asked me to rub on some cream and come back in two weeks for an exploratory check-up. Don't think I'll stick around for that!'

Clue: The rule to making and breaking this cipher is: use only the first letter of each sentence.

If you're starting to think that you might really enjoy code work, perhaps you'd be better off as a crypto-spy . . .

MAILING ADDRESS: NSA, Fort George G. Meade, Maryland, 20755-6000, USA

WEB ADDRESS: www.nsa.gov

NUMBER OF EMPLOYEES: Secret, but estimated to be 38,000 - also estimated to be a lot more than the CIA

FAST FACT: Said to be the largest employer of mathematicians in the US - and perhaps the world - NSA employees are top code-breakers and code-makers

TOP SECRET: RECRUITMENT FILE #5

NAME: Government Communications Headquarters (GCHQ)

MISSION: Employees intercept and decode information, and develop ways for the British government to transmit information securely

ESTABLISHED: 1946

LOCATION: Cheltenham, England

MAILING ADDRESS: GCHQ, Hubble Road, Cheltenham, Gloucestershire, GL51 0EX

WEB ADDRESS: www.gchq.gov.uk

NUMBER OF EMPLOYEES: More than 4,000

FAST FACT: Thanks to its shape, the new GCHQ building is nicknamed 'The Doughnut'. The main building covers the size of seventeen football pitches, with a massive garden in the middle

TOP SECRET

FAST FACT – extra!: Top GCHQ experts were once confused by strange signals sent from a transmitter in Yorkshire. Was it a new top-secret weapon being tested by a foreign spy service? Were aliens trying to get in touch? After a thorough investigation, the source of the signals was found: a sheep that liked to rub itself against the radio mast!

Of course, codes and ciphers are perfect for when you're having a conversation with someone and you want no one else to listen in. But there will be times when you'll *want* someone to overhear you and understand what you're saying. What if you're meeting an agent, who claims to have some info on Rudy, and you want Will and Damian to hear everything, without that agent knowing a thing?

Then you might wear a **wire**.

WIRES

Modern body wires are straightforward pieces of equipment. You'll have a mini microphone attached to a radio transmitter concealed somewhere – perhaps strapped to your chest. The microphone will pick up your conversation, and the transmitter will send it on to the receiver held by Will and Damian in a room, or a car, nearby. That receiver will then turn the signals back into the sounds of your voices.

SIR STEPHEN'S TOP CRYPTO-TIP:

While you want Will and Damian to listen in, you don't want anyone else to scan the airwaves and overhear – which means you'll need to encrypt the signal, even with a body wire. Your body wire system could do this automatically, scrambling your voice signal, and allowing only your colleagues to unscramble it and (hopefully) make sense of it all.

But you won't always want to transmit information using your voice. What if you're deep behind enemy lines, with General Pedro's spies all around, and you want to make sure your new knowledge about Rudy gets back to your boss safely?

One option is to send a message by old-fashioned post. But you'll still need to stop it getting into enemy hands. And one way to do this is to make your secret message very, very small . . .

MICRODOTS

These are tiny images of a secret message (which could also be in code, for extra security) or a document. They're made by taking a photo of the message and then making a minute print. The microdot can then easily be

hidden – under a postage stamp, for instance, or even by pasting it over the full stop at the end of the address on the envelope. To read the message, or make out the image, you'll need a powerful microscope.

German spies were the first to use the trick. And in 1946, J. Edgar Hoover, who was director of the US's Federal Bureau of Investigation at the time, called microdots: 'The enemy's masterpiece of espionage!'

Microdots have come on a long way since they were first used in the Second World War. Scientists recently made a microdot using some very special code indeed: DNA – the code of life. The precise order of four different building blocks of DNA inside your body determines an enormous amount about you – from the colour of your eyes, to whether you're a boy or a girl.

The modern-day microdot experts took a bit of DNA and changed the order of the building blocks very slightly, so that this DNA encrypted a message. In fact, it was a message first sent using an original microdot during the Second World War: 'June 6 Invasion: Normandy'.

They then dried the DNA, pasted it as a microdot over the full stop in a letter, posted the letter through the mail, and analysed the dot at the end. The result: they could find their message and read it perfectly!

Placing messages or images on a microdot is just one option if you're trying to use 'steganography'– made up of the Greek for 'hidden' and 'writing'. But of course there are other techniques that you can try.

HOW ABOUT INVISIBLE INK?

Invisible ink really has been used by spies. It's low-tech. But it's easy to do yourself. If you decided to use invisible ink to write a note to your boss about Rudy, you would need:

- Lemon juice for ink
- A piece of paper
- Something to write your message with
  (like a toothpick or a cotton bud)

When you've finished your note, let the paper dry and the ink will disappear. You can then post this note to your boss. They'll know to heat this mysterious piece of paper on a radiator, or even with an iron, and the words will reappear.

SIR STEPHEN'S TOP CRYPTO-TIP:

Using a normal pen or pencil, write a 'cover' message between the lines of the words you want to keep secret. That way, if any of Pedro's people intercepts the note, there'll be nothing strange about it. (People might think it suspicious if you start sending blank pieces of paper through the post!) Of course, you'll have to think about your cover message carefully. You'll have to make sure that your boss will realize there's a lot more to this letter than meets the eye – and they'll do some further investigation to look for hidden contents.

But microdots and invisible ink are certainly not the strangest methods that spies have used to conceal written messages. Sir Stephen has devoted fifty-three pages of his memoirs to this subject – here's an excerpt . . .

The Memoirs of Sir Stephen
CHAPTER 659: SWALLOW YOUR SECRETS

It's almost supper-time, and as I anticipate my habitual evening snack of caviar on toast, my thoughts turn, quite naturally, to my belly . . . So ponder this: you're a spy on the run with a secret to conceal. Where's a good spot? Where could you hide that secret so no one could find it . . . at least, not without waiting a day or two, and then some rather unpleasant investigation? The answer, of course, is your stomach!

In ancient China, spy-masters liked to write messages on silk, which they scrunched up into balls and coated with wax. Why silk? Because it will squish down very small. Why wax? To protect the message from stomach juices while it was carried to the intended recipient. Swallowing a wax-coated ball sounds disgusting, indeed. But perhaps not quite as distasteful as locating that ball at the 'other end' . . .

Chinese spies are not the only ones to think 'secrets' and 'stomachs'. Italian scientist Giovanni Porta loved food so much, he used it to carry hidden messages. But he did it using a rather clever technique. In fact, Porta worked out how to hide a message in a hard-boiled egg. The key was in the mixture he used as ink. The recipe is quite complex, but one of the most important ingredients was vinegar. When he wrote with the mix on the hard shell, the words would sink through and be left on the outside of the white part of the egg! To read the message, you'd simply break and peel away the shell, and the dark writing would be clear. Then, to destroy the message, what would you do? Eat the egg, of course. I would recommend it sliced rather thinly, with homemade mayonnaise and a dash of Worcester sauce . . .

MEDIA MESSAGES

Another option for a modern spy is to hide an encoded message in a radio broadcast or even a newspaper.

Your agency knows it could be hard to reach you directly while you're out investigating General Pedro's base. So you might arrange to tune into a particular radio wavelength at the same time every three hours . . . It's 18.00 and you grab your shortwave radio . . . And you hear a broadcast about farming practices in Kenya. This isn't one of the pre-arranged programmes that would mean either 'return immediately' or 'launch a mission against Pedro's base'. So you'll have to wait until tomorrow to see if any instructions will come through . . .

How would you send and receive messages with a newspaper? Well, you could always use the small ads.

Scan this section of any national newspaper and you might find:

> WANTED: one eighteenth-century Mongolian brass-handled bed-pan with mother-of-pearl inlay. Will pay $2,000. REPLY TODAY.'

Could be genuine? Could be. Or it might be code offering an agent money if they make contact.

So how would they do it? Face-to-face meetings are always risky. One way to get regular instructions to an agent and to get information in return is to set up a **drop**.

NOTEBOOK OF SPENCER BING

DAY: Monday
TIME: 13.55
LOCATION: Greenwich, London
BACKGROUND: Got a call to meet a man with 'intel'
in a pub. Man looked familiar but couldn't place
him. Dark glasses. White beard. Told me he had
crucial info about Felix Flashmonger, my rival at
the Daily Dossier. Wouldn't reveal full details
in the pub. Told me he'd let me know where to go
for more. This morning: a letter in the post. A
single sentence: 'Greenwich, fourth park bench in
from the gates, on the left.' This afternoon: an
email. Two words: 'Two o'clock.'

I've spotted the bench. Taken the precaution of
procuring a neighbour's dog. Good cover, I
thought. Only trouble is: dog won't keep to
heel. I'm shouting, it's barking and everyone's
looking . . . Approaching bench. Bench clear.
Sitting down on bench. Dog going crazy, foaming
at the mouth. I'm reaching under the bench,
pretending to be tying up dog. Aha. I've found
something. I'm retrieving a package . . . It's
an envelope. Taped shut. I'm opening it . . . A
sheet of paper. And it reads:

'CRUCIAL INFORMATION: FELIX FLASHMONGER IS A
FAR BETTER REPORTER THAN YOU'LL EVER BE!
SIGNED: FELIX FLASHMONGER.'

The dark glasses! The white beard! A cunning disguise! It was Felix all along!

In fact, arrangements to leave information at an arranged spot – a drop – at regular times are often made between intelligence officers and their agents. That spot needn't be under a park bench, of course. It could be in a post box. Or in a tree trunk hollow. Even a rubbish bin. As long as the drop zone is kept under close observation at the arranged times, the officer will always be able to collect the latest news, or post new instructions, without any need for face-to-face meetings.

But if you must have a face-to-face meeting, how will you recognize your contact if you've never met before?

What if you get a message from HQ to leave the field and head straight to New Delhi to meet an undercover agent working for the SIS? She apparently has some 'news' about Rudy. You've been told to meet her at the central railway station, at the entrance to platform one, at midday. You know this: she's got black hair, brown eyes and she'll be wearing jeans and a pink top.

The clothing tip will help cut your chances of getting the wrong person. But if you spot someone matching that description, you need to know they're really the agent – and not a foreign spy who's somehow found out about the meet, done away with the agent, and come to meet you in her place.

One popular method is to use a password. You'll probably have seen this in a movie. The password needn't be a single word – it could be a conversation. The agreed lines could run like this:

YOU: Good morning, do you happen to know if the 14.42 to Jaipur is running today?

WOMAN IN PINK TOP: I believe it was cancelled. Leaves on the line, don't you know?

YOU: What a shame! And I was so looking forward to the trip. My old aunt lives there – has a house with two dozen cats.

(To anyone overhearing, this could be a genuine conversation – but the content is exactly as pre-arranged. Now you can move away from the clock – and she can talk.)

WOMAN IN PINK TOP: Rudy had a meet with some guy in southern China four days before you saw him at Pedro's base. One of our agents is working on another case with a Chinese connection and saw the surveillance shots. Rudy is definitely in the background.

AHA!

But what if a foreign spy agency had somehow intercepted the message containing details of the password-conversation that you'd sent to the agent? Then another woman could still have taken your agent's place.

Yet another method of identifying contacts could be to use a stash of banknotes torn roughly in half. Your HQ would keep one set of halves, and securely distribute the other set to bases around the world. Each half would be marked with an invisible ink identifier. Then you could take one of the halves with you on the plane, send a message with the identifier to the New Delhi office, and make sure the agent that turned up had another half that matched *exactly*.

Those are just a few options for making sure the person you're meeting really is who you think they are. See if you can come up with any others.

Then, when you've done that, it's time for some instruction in how to gather intelligence in the first place. It's no use knowing how to pass on information securely if you have nothing to transmit. So how do spies find out secrets?

One of the most important answers is: **surveillance**.

When you were watching Rudy with those night-vision binoculars, you were engaged in surveillance. This basically means snooping on your target – whether it's a person, a group or even a company. Do it badly, and you'll be captured. To do it well, you'll need some intensive training in techniques and special gadgets. Turn the page now to find out more . . .

CHAPTER 3

THE ART OF SURVEILLANCE

SURVEILLANCE IS ONE OF A SPY'S MOST IMPORTANT TASKS – AND YOU MUST DO IT WITHOUT RAISING YOUR TARGET'S SUSPICIONS.

There are two main approaches.

Close-quarter surveillance. You'll follow a target on foot or in a vehicle.

Remote surveillance. You'll use long-distance tracking devices, spy satellites, computer monitoring equipment and other gadgets to keep track of their activities.

In this chapter, you'll learn all you need to know about the first sort: getting close – and not getting noticed.

```
TO: OUR TOP AGENT

FROM: HQ

RICHARD 'RUDY' RAWCUS IS ON HIS WAY TO LONDON
POINT OF ORIGIN: SOUTH-EAST ASIA
OBJECTIVE: LOCATE RUDY AND FOLLOW TO HIS CONTACT
```

So, it's 06.00 hours, mid-winter, and you're at the arrivals zone in Heathrow Airport, on the lookout for Rudy. You have this intelligence:

- You spotted old Rudy outside the remote base and missile dump belonging to General Pedro, the crazy arms dealer. At the time Rudy was supposed to be on holiday in Antigua

- You know Rudy was in southern China a few days before that rendezvous with Pedro – but you don't yet know the purpose of either trip

- Rudy's bank balance has been checked. It stands at more than one million pounds. He'd never make that on a secret-service salary

- Rudy has told his boss he'll be late returning to work from holiday – he's been called away to visit a 'sick aunt' in London

The SIS suspects that Rudy is heading to England for a secret meet.

So, you're waiting at the airport with Damian and Will. Will is pretending to browse magazines at a news-stand. Damian is pretending to be a black-cab driver. He's parked outside, along with six other agents in three other cabs, waiting for your cue.

Rudy's seen you before, of course – in fact, he knows you well. So to spot and tail him without him knowing, you'll need an excellent disguise.

COVER-UP!
What's the best way to disguise yourself? You'd better get it right or you'll be in big trouble.

Let's start with the basics.

Some things are easy to change. If you don't wear glasses, you can put on a pair. If you do, you can take them off. If you have blond hair, you can dye it brown. If you have blue eyes, you can wear brown contact lenses. That's the easy stuff.

But there are other things that will give you away.

Most spies who work in the field are ordinary looking – the kind of people you'd pass on the street and not even notice. There's little about them that stands out. This also means that changing their hair colour or their clothes is much more likely to be an effective disguise than it would on a person seven feet tall with a broken nose, braces and a limp.

With Rudy, of course, there's a special problem – he knows what you look like already. Let's say for a moment that you're an unusual spy with a distinguishing feature – a very large nose. You can't easily cover this up. But you can distract people's attention. CIA experts would be keen to do it with something else very noticeable – like a large set of gold platings for your teeth.

So if you're in disguise, with different coloured hair and a moustache, perhaps, and Rudy sees you, the first thing he notices won't be your nose, but the set of gold teeth. This should reduce the risk that he'll recognize you as being you.

If you're not convinced, there's another option for transforming your face. It's secret work, and there's little known about it, other than its name ...

DAGGER

One former disguise expert at the CIA says his team developed total facial 'masks' that you can wear to completely transform your face – so much so that you look like a completely different person. According to this officer, one of his colleagues briefed a former US president for more than half an hour, without him knowing who she really was – then she peeled off her mask to reveal her true identity!

But what if you could go one step further? What if you could become ... invisible?

In the film *Die Another Day*, James Bond drives an Aston Martin that he can make temporarily invisible. In fact, researchers really are working on a way to make cars – and even people – disappear. How? It all relies on cameras. Spencer Bing visited a Japanese research lab to find out more ...

TIME: 09.00
LOCATION: Japan

I'm standing in a laboratory
that's packed with people.

I'm looking at a man. I've
touched him, prodded him in the stomach, poked
him in the leg.
He squealed.
CONCLUSION 1: he's human
CONCLUSION 2: he's alive

He's wearing a luminous yellow jacket. And now
he's activating a camera and projection system.
I've been told to watch his belly. And I am . . .
And now I'm not! It's gone! I can see straight
through him. Someone's walking behind him — and
I can see them move!

The idea behind the technology is simple. Cameras take
pictures of what's happening behind the person who wants
to be made 'invisible'. These pictures are then projected on
to the front of their body. So it seems as though you're
looking straight through them!

**But this work is at an early stage. At the moment, it wouldn't
really convince anyone. Except maybe Spencer Bing.**

At least this means that old Rudy Rawcus won't be able to
sneak invisibly into Heathrow. But he is a top agent. He

knows his stuff. And that means that he'll probably also be in disguise. As well as being able to transform yourself, you'll need to be able to identify targets who don't want to be recognized . . .

06.20 HOURS. A man enters the arrivals zone. He's the same height as Rudy, and there's something about his face that's familiar. But he's got a bushy moustache, and white-blond hair, and he's wearing a backpack and carrying a guide to England written in German . . .

Could this backpacker really be Rudy?

One way to check would be to use a 'biometric' test. These are tests based on patterns in parts of the body – like the iris (the coloured part of your eye) or the ridges that make up a fingerprint.

If MI6 files already contained an image of Rudy's iris, you could take a new scan and compare the two. But how can you do that when he's on the move – and the last thing you want is for him to notice you?

In fact, the CIA is working on handheld devices that can quickly scan the iris of a person walking by. The device would then compare this image with others in its database. If you got a match, you'd know whether the 'blond' with the bushy moustache really is Rudy.

Another alternative could be to come up with a reason for checking the fingerprints of everyone coming off the flight that morning – **additional security**, you could call it. Then you could use a computer to check the SIS records and identify your man.

But could Rudy get around these tests? If he was well prepared, he could.

- It's easy enough to make false fingerprints from thin pieces of sticky plastic. Scientists have even made fake prints that have tricked security systems

- If Rudy's wearing coloured contact lenses, that iris recognition system will be no use whatsoever

So, fingerprint detection and iris recognition aren't looking too promising. But remember: you know Rudy well. And you know that some things, like height and weight, are harder to disguise. Let's say you decide that this 'German' really is your old pal – and he hasn't noticed you.

What do you do?

1. Alert Will, who's still at the news-stand, and Damian, in the taxi outside. You know from Chapter 2 that you'll be wearing a mini-microphone and a tiny earpiece so the three of you can stay in touch. But make sure you don't:

    a. *Stop moving and stare into space when Will replies*
    b. *Fiddle with your earpiece*

Those are two clear giveaways to anyone watching that you're wearing a communications system.

2. Start to trail Rudy. This is a dangerous time. You'll have to make full use of your elite training to follow him without him spotting you.

 Try this quiz to see how good you'd really be:

1. What should you do if Rudy glances around?
   a. *Duck behind the nearest escalator*
   b. *Immediately pretend to be doing up a shoelace*
   c. *Carry on walking*

2. When trailing Rudy:
   a. *Don't do anything even vaguely out of the ordinary – act like everyone else in the airport*
   b. *Use structures around you for cover*
   c. *Hold out your ID card to make people move out of the way*

3. If Rudy suddenly stops walking, you should:
   a. *Stop as well*
   b. *Walk past him*
   c. *Turn around and walk in the other direction*

Answers:

1. c – or maybe b. Definitely not a. Rudy would be very likely to notice this unusual behaviour. You could hide your face by pretending to be doing up a shoelace or

pulling up a sock – but use this trick only once. If every time Rudy glances behind him, he sees the same person bending over, he'll be suspicious.

2. b. Of course, it's important that you blend in with the crowd. And luckily, there's a good mix of people at an airport. If you keep hold of a briefcase and Will carries an overnight bag, you're less likely to stand out. BUT you should not behave just like everyone else at the airport. In fact, you should be using any natural cover available – walk behind car-rental kiosks or on the other side of an escalator from Rudy, while still keeping an eye on him.

3. If you can, a. If not, b. Constantly look ahead for options if Rudy suddenly does something unexpected, like stopping in his tracks. You can't just stop in the middle of the airport as well – it would be far too obvious. But if there's a wire rack holding hotel brochures ahead, and he passes it then stops dead, you can easily pretend that you were making a beeline for those brochures all along.

But if you're right behind Rudy when he suddenly stops, keep walking – even if it means you have to go right past him. Will is also following and you can walk into the toilets, use your body communications system to check with Will when Rudy's on the move again – and then head back out to continue your surveillance. (You could even take advantage of the cover of a toilet cubicle to quickly change your disguise – reducing the risk that Rudy will spot you when you re-emerge.)

While you're following Rudy, you'll need to gather all the info you can. Perhaps the backpacker disguise is one of his favourites, so it would be useful if you could take a snapshot of him for later use. And what if he stops in the airport to talk to someone? You'll need to make a record, just in case that someone is an important contact. Of course, you can't whip out your camera and ask Rudy and his 'friend' to say 'cheese' … so what could you do?

Well, you could use a video spy-camera so small it can be sewn into clothes. You can arrange these lightweight cameras so that the tiny lens is attached to your tie – or peeking through a hole in your briefcase. As you follow Rudy it will digitally record everything he does.

Or you could choose a combined camera-microphone spy pen. These pens look and work just like the real thing – but stick one in your shirt pocket, and it will record and transmit pictures and sound to a receiver that could be kept by Damian outside in the cab.

You could even choose a pair of sunglasses that contain a minute digital camera (the hole for the lens is so small no one walking by would see it). These glasses also feature a tiny computer display screen on the left lens, which you could use to check the latest emailed instructions from HQ. (But you won't be able to wear your rear-view glasses and special sunglasses at the same time! And beware: sunglasses worn indoors automatically make you stand out.)

Of course, secret cameras have been around for some time. Sir Stephen devotes 212 pages of his memoirs to his surveillance recollections . . . Which of the following do you think were genuine gadgets?

1. *Book-camera*
2. *Thermos flask-camera*
3. *Button-camera*

Answers:

Sir Stephen:

1. Indeed! The Tessina was a delightfully mini Swiss-made 35mm film camera. And one rather popular way to conceal it was to cut a chunk out of the inside of a book and slot the camera inside. When the book was closed, the lens would peep out through a hole in the pages. By pressing on the book's cover, one could take a secret picture.

2. Unlikely but true! You might have thought us Brits would have been the ones to take tea-drinking to another level but in fact the Thermos flask-camera was the invention of the

KGB, feared spy organization of the former Soviet Union. Those clever gadget-makers fitted a mini-camera inside a normal Thermos flask. The lens was fitted in the centre of the base, with a hidden button on the side for taking a picture. So, dear readers, beware old ladies with flasks, pouring cups of tea. They might not be all they seem . . .

3. I confirm it! This was another smart Russian idea. The camera was concealed in the lining of a jacket and its lens was covered with what appeared to be a normal button. To take a picture, you'd squeeze a controller in your pocket, and that fake button would briefly open up! The only downside was that its usefulness was rather limited on a hot day, when anyone in a jacket would stand out a mile. In fact, one really did require a cold snap to take a snap . . .

But enough of the past. Back to the present.

FAST FORWARD

You and Will are doing well. You've kept Rudy in your sights and he hasn't spotted you. Now he's made it outside the airport terminal and he's hailing a black cab. It's your turn to do the same – only Damian is ready and waiting . . .

Using a local taxi cab, rather than a car, is a good choice for road surveillance. There will be so many black cabs on the road into the city from Heathrow, it won't seem strange to Rudy if he sees one repeatedly in the rear-view mirror. But of course Rudy could take a note of the number plate – and he might start to get suspicious if you're constantly behind him.

This is where the six other agents in the other three cabs come in.

Four spy-cabs are much better than one. And this is how you might organize them:

1. First, make sure you have at least two people in each surveillance vehicle. One will be the driver, the other the navigator. Each cab will take a turn at keeping a close eye on Rudy – and the cab on the job will be known as the Command Vehicle.

2. The navigator in the Command Vehicle must concentrate on reading the map, updating the other spy-cabs on their exact location, and taking surveillance pictures, if necessary. The driver must follow the target (Rudy). If possible, have at least one other car between you and your target.

3. The other three vehicles will be waiting to spring into action. You might choose to have a second vehicle also following behind Rudy. But this cab will stay further back in the traffic, until you give a signal for it to take over your position. If you've been close behind Rudy for a while, and then take a turn-off when he carries on straight ahead, he'll lose any suspicions that you're following him – and it'll take some time before he notices a new cab on his tail.

4. Set up two spy-cabs at locations along the route you think Rudy might follow. If you think he's likely to head into the city, you could station spy-cabs three and four at junctions on the road in from Heathrow. These cabs could

take over the job of following Rudy, while cab number two leaves to join you at a meeting spot. Again, this is likely to put Rudy's mind at rest.

So, you've done your bit, and spy-cab four has picked up Rudy's tail. Thanks to info from the navigator, you know their location – and you've switched to another car and are in hot pursuit. You want to be there when Rudy finally comes to a stop!

And there he is! Rudy's taxi is turning a corner . . . and now it's coming to a halt and he's getting out.

You're in the East End. You park and, through your high-powered binoculars, you watch Rudy enter an office block and then appear in a window on the third floor.

He sits down at a desk, boots up a computer and starts to type. Then, from a door at the far side of the room, a man emerges. You know him at once. It's General Pedro! But what's he doing here? And what are they up to? *What are they saying?*

Your close-quarter surveillance is at an end. Now it's time to use long-distance techniques to learn all you can about Rudy Rawcus and his secret deals. To learn how, look at Chapter 4.

CHAPTER 4
DISTANCE IS NO OBJECT

MIDNIGHT: YOU'RE ON FOOT, HIDING IN THE SHADOWS OUTSIDE THAT EAST END OFFICE BLOCK

The lights are off. Rudy's in a makeshift bedroom next to his office for the night. And it's time for you and your team to set up the surveillance kit.

How will you do it?

First, you'll get the blueprints to the building from the local planning department. This will show you the layout – how many rooms you'll have to deal with, and the fastest ways in and out.

SIR STEPHEN'S TOP TIP:

Maps are vital to spies. Often, you'll be called on to make maps of secret HQs that you've penetrated for other spies to use. It's worth practising your map-making skills as often as possible. Next time you visit a house for the first time, try to memorize the layout and make a map of it when you get home. Or, get a piece of paper and a pen right now and see if you can draw a map of your school from memory, showing all the rooms, stairs and corridors.

Now, back to the East End office block . . .

You've scanned the blueprints. You've worked out how to slip straight into the office, and straight back out. These are your options for remote surveillance.

VISION

Spies have hundreds of camera-equipped gadgets to choose from. You might decide to swap the plain office clock on the wall for one that looks just the same – except it also contains a tiny wide-angle lens.

'CLICK!'

'Wide-angle' means you'll get a good amount of width in your picture. Hopefully, you'll get a view of the entire width of the room.

If there's a mirror fixed above Rudy's desk, you could replace that regular mirror with a special sort of plastic that looks just the same. But you can put a mini-camera behind that 'mirror' and it will see right through.

SOUND

To eavesdrop on Rudy, you can install bugs inside the office itself. Not the creepy-crawly kind, of course. These bugs are little devices that pick up sound and send it through the air to a receiver. This receiver might be in an innocent-looking 'plumber's' van parked outside the apartment block. Often, these bugs will use radio waves to do the job.

Your most important task when placing a bug is to make sure it's well hidden. Behind a picture frame or the underside of a chair could be good spots to choose.

SIR STEPHEN'S TOP TIP:
I'll say it again: practice makes perfect. Take a look around the room you're in right now. Try to pick ten places that you think could be perfect for hiding bugs. This kind of practice will help when you're on the job.

You might also want to place a bug in a phone handset, so you can listen in on any calls.

But what if the blueprints show that it'll be tricky to get into that office without making a lot of noise close to where Rudy's asleep? The last thing you want to do is wake him up.

In this case, one option could be to 'borrow' the floor above or below and drill (with a special reduced-noise drill) a few small holes into the office. Then you'll be able to insert **fibrescopes**. These are the sorts of gadget used by doctors when they want to take a good look at your insides. Instead of inserting a bendy tube with a camera on the end into someone's stomach, you'll push its tip through the floorboards or the ceiling, into Rudy's office, and wiggle it about until you get a perfect view of the room. If you drill up underneath a piece of furniture with legs – like a table – there's much less chance that someone will notice your fibrescope. You can also attach a tiny microphone to listen in on Rudy's conversations.

But while fibrescopes can certainly be useful, it isn't necessary to enter the office block to gather intelligence on Rudy.

From your surveillance van, you could use a camera with a

long-distance zoom lens. And you could use a super-powerful 'directional' microphone, which will let you home in on a conversation across the street. If the window to Rudy's office is open, you could sit in a window in the building opposite and use one of these microphones to listen to his conversations. But you'll have to hope he doesn't spot you.

Or you could secretly bug the room – without putting any actual equipment inside it. How?

Insider journalist Spencer Bing persuaded a spy gadget guru to spill the beans on the very latest technology . . .

TIME: Late
LOCATION: A back alley, London

I'm standing in the shadows waiting
for Dr X. He refuses to tell me his real name.
But he will tell me the secret to bugging a room
— remotely. And there's a noise ... I can hear
footsteps. It's a man in a long black cloak,
wearing a baseball cap and dark glasses!

ME: Dr X?

DR X (hissing): Who do you think?

ME: Righto. What can you tell me about
remote bugging?

DR X: I can tell you this: you sit in the back of a surveillance van. This van can be parked up to half a kilometre away from the room you want to bug. OK?

ME: OK so far.

DR X: Then, you must know that a window vibrates a tiny amount when someone inside is talking — and the vibrations are different, depending on the words being spoken. Using a special camera, you'll direct a beam of infrared light at the closed window. The beam hits the window — and bounces back. A computer system analyses the beam that returns and can tell what vibrations there were in the window pane — and so what was being said. It turns the vibration information back into words and records the whole conversation.

ME: That's amazing!

DR X: Amazing but true. Now I've said enough.

And he's gone. And I have the secret to remote bugging!

TECHNICAL NOTE: You can't usually see infrared (IR) 'light' – but you probably use it every day. How? Your TV remote control communicates with the TV set using an IR beam.

So, now you're set up for basic sound and vision surveillance. But there are other ways to gather vital information.

DISC-GRACEFUL!

What was Rudy typing after he booted up that computer? Was he accessing a website? Sending an email? There are easy ways to find out . . .

Spencer Bing has compiled his own list of top techniques for sneaking info from other people's computers. (He's hoping to use some of them to steal his rival Felix Flashmonger's exclusive stories and publish them as his own . . .)

```
1. KEYSTROKE MONITORING SOFTWARE
Sneaky rating: ***
Anyone can buy software that records all
activity on a computer and then forwards the
details to them. Some software will
automatically send on a record of every single
key that is pressed, as well as the content of
emails and even web-based chats. But there is
one catch — you need to get that software on to
their computer in the first place.
SOLUTION: Spies can use computer viruses to
secretly do this
```

2. MONITOR RADIATION

Sneaky rating: *****

This radiation is produced by electronic parts
inside computer monitors. Using an antenna and
a receiver, a spy in a van outside could
capture this radiation — and use it to work
out the exact images or words that were shown
on the screen!

3. MONITOR FLICKER

Sneaky rating: *****!

Another brilliant way of reading a monitor
screen — even if it's facing away from you!
This clever technique is based on the pattern
of light that comes from the screen. A computer
can take this light — and tell you what's
actually on the screen at the time. And this
works even if the computer gets the light after
it's been reflected back from a wall or has
passed through a curtain. You could be sitting
in a room in a building across the street, and
use a telescope to gather the necessary light
info.

4. WIRELESS INTERCEPTION

Sneaky rating: **

Wireless networks are getting much more popular
in offices and homes. Instead of connecting a
computer to the internet or to another computer
using cables, information is sent through the
air. What could be easier than waiting outside

the office — and using your laptop to intercept
the data?

5. HARD-DRIVE SEARCH
Sneaky rating: **
'Clean' hard drives. Many people think that once
they've hit 'delete' on a file, that file
vanishes from their hard drive — but it doesn't.
Students at the prestigious Massachusetts
Institute of Technology in the United States
looked at more than 150 second-hand hard drives,
and found more than 6,000 credit card numbers! In
fact, 'deleting' a file doesn't usually wipe it —
it just deletes the 'tag' that points to that
file. But if you're a computer whizz, you can
still find it. So if Rudy really wants to remove
all contacts from the hard drive of his computer
once he's done with it, the best way to do it is
to completely fill it with other data.

Now it's time to review your surveillance checklist.

SOUND

VISION

COMPUTERS

But are you missing something here? What about faxes?
What if your monitor flicker surveillance fails to collect a

vital email? Well, there is another service that you, as a spy, can turn to. Its name is **Echelon**.

NAME: Echelon. A global eavesdropping network. It can reportedly intercept almost any electronic communication. That includes emails, mobile phone calls, web page downloads, faxes, normal phone conversations and even satellite transmissions

RUN BY: Intelligence organizations of the US (which takes the lead), UK, Canada, Australia and New Zealand

ESTABLISHED: The first Echelon network was set up in 1971

But *how* does Echelon do it? *How* can it listen in on billions of phone calls?

Let's go back to phone tapping for a moment. As you already know, one way to listen in on someone's phone calls is to put a bug in their handset. But in fact you can intercept a phone call at any point along the cables that connect your phone

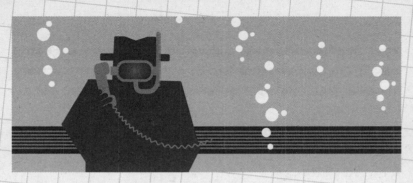

to the one used by the person you're talking to. If you place that 'tap' on the deep underwater cables that carry phone calls between continents, you can monitor tens of thousands of phone calls at once.

But isn't that a *huge* waste of time? After all, you've listened to your parents on the phone – you know how dull their conversations with your relatives can be. Who'd want to listen to zillions of chats about what someone's having for tea and how their back's a bit sore, on the off-chance of spotting a real threat to national security?

Of course, this doesn't really happen. Exactly how Echelon works is secret. But it's thought to use automatic systems to look out for key words in phone calls or emails – like 'bomb'!

But if the bugs in your East End office block revealed Rudy discussing an operation referred to only as 'Operation Esmeralda', you could then use the Echelon service to keep a lookout for anyone, anywhere in the world, using that same phrase. And what if it found someone . . .?

What if you got the news that a man on a satellite phone in southern China had been in touch with Rudy? (Could this have been the man that Rudy met before heading off to Pedro's base?) Their conversation had contained the words 'nuclear', 'disaster' and 'Operation Esmeralda'. What would you do?

You'd go in for a closer look, of course.

EYE IN THE SKY

When it comes to remote surveillance, some types are more remote than others.

Aeroplanes and satellites are both used to gather pictures of targets located anywhere on the surface of the Earth.

TOP SECRET: / TECHNOLOGY REPORT #2

SPYPLANES: aka UAVs (Unmanned Aerial Vehicles)

ADVANCED EXAMPLE:
SiMiCon RotorCraft (SRC), developed by engineers in Norway. This saucer-shaped, unmanned craft takes off like a helicopter – and flies like a plane

Remote-control UAVs have been brilliant at gathering images for intelligence agencies. But the United States has gone even further. It has built unmanned spyplanes that also fire missiles. The 'Predator' spyplane was developed for 'reconnaissance' (gathering and sending back information), but it has also been used to fire at enemy targets

TECHNICAL NOTE: Although UAVs don't have a crew on board, they're still flown by human pilots. The pilot stays on the ground and remotely controls the spyplane

TECHNOLOGY REPORT #3

NAME: Imagery Intelligence (IMINT) Satellites. These *space* satellites use cameras and radar to produce sharp pictures of targets on the ground

ADVANCED EXAMPLE: The United States KH military satellites can home in on an object measuring just ten centimetres across. So if you're sitting outside, one of these satellites could spot this book in your hand

Some satellites can even see in the dark – so while your neighbour might not be able to spot you sitting in the garden at midnight, a satellite could!

Now, from the super high-tech to the low-tech.

A comprehensive surveillance operation will also investigate the target's mail. Which means you'll need to sneak a peak at whatever post gets shoved through Rudy's office block letterbox.

Reading other people's mail has a long history.

The Memoirs of Sir Stephen
CHAPTER 612: GHOST POST

Ah, I remember it well. June of 1942, and from an undercover role as a minor member of the Royal Family, I was switched to an altogether different sort of task. My new challenge was to pretend to be a postman with the Royal Mail, and to read all correspondence destined for Lady Joy Chapman, of Sloane Square, Chelsea – society hostess and suspected German spy.

To assist me, I had what was the very latest in letter interception technology: the Letter Removal Device. Simple system, once one had the knack. Wooden handle with two long skewers attached. Wind-up mechanism in the base. Simply insert skewers through open gap of the envelope, above the seal, slipping one on either side of the fold in the letter inside. Turn mechanism and the skewers rotate, winding the letter around them, tighter and tighter. Simple then, to remove skewers plus letter, read letter, rewind letter around the old gadget and reinsert into envelope, with glue still intact!

Of course, now there are more high-tech alternatives. Modern spies can use a spray that makes the envelope see-through for a short time. So you'll be able to read what's inside, without opening it up or removing the letter at all.

Now, from low-tech . . . to lower-than-low-tech. As well as checking the mail, you'll also need to check the rubbish bins. In fact, spy agencies set a lot of store by sorting through rubbish. It can tell you more than you might think about a person, from what kind of food they like to eat, to where they were the previous Friday night.

OK, so you're unlikely to find an invoice reading:

```
TO: General Pedro
FROM: Rudy Rawcus
AMOUNT DUE: Half a million pounds
FOR: Secret services rendered
```

But you might find an air ticket, or a bank statement, or a map – all things that might be important in your investigation.

FIGHTING BACK!

So, now you know how to set up surveillance on Rudy. Easy.

But wait . . . Rudy's an expert, so he's bound to know all about these types of spying technology. And, annoyingly for you, there are hundreds of gadgets out there to protect your communications as well as to let you know if someone's spying on you. Here are just a few examples of **counter-surveillance**:

1. Bug detectors

Rudy probably has a little bug-detecting box in his pocket. These devices detect the types of radio transmissions produced by bugs or body wires. And they can be set up so that you won't even know if Rudy's on to you. If he feels the gadget vibrating, he'll know he's being overheard – and he might start feeding you fake information to put you on the wrong track.

2. Keystroke detectors

Yes, as well as software to snoop on your computer use, you can buy software to sound the alarm if someone's trying to sneak information from your system.

3. Camera detectors

Hand-held scanners can pick up the activity of a hidden video camera.

4. Telephone protectors

Rudy might well have a phone-protection device fitted. These systems can not only alert you if someone's tampered with the phone, they can also change the signal that's sent down the line. The aim is to make it much harder for anyone listening in to understand what you're saying.

5. A shielded tent

Yes, really – a tent. But not the sort you'd go camping in. These special tents stop radio waves getting in or out. So if Rudy wants a guaranteed secret conversation, he could go inside the tent – and your bugs won't be able to listen in. And Rudy could shift his computer inside the tent, preventing you from detecting what's on the screen. It's a crude method of deflecting spy-attacks – but it works! In fact, the shielded tent idea is the basis for the 'clean rooms' that you'll have in your spy HQ. These rooms stop all radio waves and electromagnetic signals getting in or out. So if you're in there for a meeting with your boss, you'll know you can reveal all without enemies listening in.

So, surveillance isn't perfect. In some ways, it's a battle of wits between you and the person you're trying to monitor. What if Rudy discovers a bug, realizes you're on to him and tries to scarper from that office block? And what if you're forced to CATCH HIM before you've had a chance to learn what on earth Operation Esmeralda is really all about?

Then you'll need your top spy psychology training to get to the truth . . .

CHAPTER 5

MIND CONTROL

CLASSIFIED

THINK YOU'RE A BIT OF A WHIZZ AT SPOTTING A LIE? THINK YOU COULD SPOT A DOUBLE-CROSSING AGENT LYING ABOUT HIS CONTACTS?

Well, take this test and find out.

1. When someone's lying to you, they're likely to:
   a. use short sentences
   b. go on for ages

2. A fibber is more likely to:
   a. look you right in the eye
   b. avoid eye contact

3. Don't believe a word from someone who:
   a. fidgets
   b. stands very still

Answers:

1. a. Yes, people who are lying are more likely to talk in short, sharp sentences.
2. a. To pretend they're being honest and truthful, someone who's lying will actually spend more time looking at you right in the eye than someone who's telling the truth.
3. b. Again, people know that fidgeting is supposed to be a sign of being less than honest, so liars are more likely to keep very still.

FAST FACT: People who often have 'gut instincts' about things are actually worse at detecting liars. (And, according to one study, police officers and people who operate lie detectors are no better than the average person at spotting people spouting fibs.)

But you have no choice: you have to interrogate fellow spy Rudy Rawcus, who knows all there is to know about how to lie convincingly. What's the best way to get to the truth?

One technique favoured by American officers in particular is the lie-detector test.

Spencer Bing found out first-hand how it works.

You sit down in a chair and a neat assistant attaches sensors to your body. These sensors detect your pulse, your blood pressure, how much you're sweating and how fast you're breathing.

BING: (Gulp!)

You're asked two or three straightforward questions.

TESTER: Is your name Spencer Bing?
BING: Er . . . you mean really?
TESTER: Yes, really!
BING: Er . . . no.
ASSISTANT (checking readout): He's telling the truth.
TESTER: Let's try something simpler: are you a man?
BING (relieved): Yes.
ASSISTANT: A OK.
TESTER: Now the real questions begin. Are you a top reporter?
BING (dejected): No.
(Assistant smiles.)

People who give others lie-detector tests are usually very well trained. They're supposed to look for particular combinations of giveaway factors, like a spurt in your heart rate and a whoosh of sweat when you're lying.

But one company has even developed a pair of glasses with an inbuilt lie detector! This system analyses voices to pick up stress. The system needs software running on a computer to do the analysis – but you could keep the computer in your pocket, with a link to the glasses. The company says that small lights on the inside of your glasses will flash continually if the person you're talking to is telling the truth.

Not all scientists think that these sorts of lie-detector systems are reliable though. They say that some people might seem to be lying, when in fact they're telling the truth, but they're stressed for some other reason – maybe because they're afraid of being interrogated!

So if a lie detector isn't going to be much use, what else could you try?

You could always go for the classic spy solution: the truth serum . . .

The Memoirs of Sir Stephen
CHAPTER 749: THE TRUTH SERUM

Makes me shiver to think of it, but once upon a time, I, Sir Stephen, was given the dreaded injection. It was a cold, dark night in Moscow. And I was in a cold, dark cell – with the dastardly Russian spymaster, Kremlinski. Easy to identify, he could never look at you straight, always squinting with his right eye. Kremlinski insisted I reveal the whereabouts of three of our top men. Naturally, I refused. He asked again. Once more, I refused. He asked again . . . This went on for some time.

Then the door to my cell opened. I strained my tired, dark-accustomed eyes and saw the pale, grim face of a nurse. She wore a smart white outfit and an evil smile. In one hand, the key to my cell. In the other, a gleaming syringe. Kremlinski faced me: 'This is it, Sir Stephen. You will keep your secrets no longer. With this quick injection, the truth will be mine!'

How did I respond? Well, I'm pleased to report, I handled this chemical challenge like the top intelligence officer I undoubtedly was. The nurse gave me the jab, and slowly, but surely, I began to feel sleepy. My heart started to slow. My mind clouded. My head felt weak.

I mustered my energy and looked Kremlinski right in the eye. And I laughed. 'Always meant to tell you, old chap: you must do something about that terrible squint!' I rolled around in my chair (or as much as my manacled state would permit).

'Tell me where they are!' he thundered.

'Tell the nurse she's a hag!' I cried.

And just a few minutes after that awful needle was plunged into my arm, my muddle-headedness was over. My mind cleared. And I saw Kremlinski staring glumly at his shoes, one hand over his bad eye, the other holding back the nurse. I had been given the serum, and I'd kept my secrets and survived!

In fact, the 'truth serum' can't make anyone tell the truth against their wishes. The drug, also known as sodium pentothal, is a sedative. In other words, it makes people sleepy. It's even used as an anaesthetic for hospital operations.

In small doses, it can make people more talkative and so more likely to blurt things out. But it can't force anyone to reveal something they're determined to keep secret.

So, the lie detector's looking dodgy, the truth serum's unlikely to work . . . Apart from your training in spotting the body language of a liar, what else could you use to interrogate Rudy and tell fact from fiction?

GETTING WARMER . . .

One hot idea could be to use a special camera that monitors the temperature of his face.

These 'thermal' cameras can pick up the heat associated with a sudden rush of blood to the area around the eyes – a strange physical change that has been linked to lying.

Alternatively, you might try a brain scan – American scientists have found that when someone is lying, there are bursts of activity in certain parts of their brain – and specialized scanners can pick this up.

Another possible option is hypnosis.

YOU ARE GETTING SLEEPY . . .

Experts argue about whether hypnosis works or not. Mostly, they argue because they don't understand *how* it might work. But some people do seem to be susceptible to being put in a 'hypnotic trance'. And once they're there, they become more suggestible – and, some spy-masters think, more likely to tell the truth.

Hypnotists use lots of different methods for putting people into a trance.

One popular way is to get a person to breathe very deeply and imagine themselves moving down a set of steps – and with each step they're getting closer to a safe place where they feel calm and relaxed . . .

Still awake? Good!

Because if none of these methods work, you'll have to use psychological 'tricks' to get Rudy to talk.

When you're questioning him about his links with General Pedro and his nuclear knowledge, you should try to think of ways to catch him out.

TRANSCRIPT OF INTERVIEW WITH 'RUDY' RAWCUS.
21 SEPTEMBER. 07.00.

YOU: SO, RUDY, WHO INTRODUCED YOU TO PEDRO?

RUDY: I met him at a party in London! I got up to
sing a song. He liked it. He invited me out to Asia
to sing!

YOU: WHAT SONG WERE YOU SINGING AT THIS PARTY?

RUDY: 'Who Wants to Live Forever?'

TRANSCRIPT OF INTERVIEW WITH 'RUDY' RAWCUS.
21 SEPTEMBER. 23.45.

YOU: WHERE DID YOU STAY IN ASIA?

RUDY: I told you, in the guest wing at the general's
house.

YOU: AND WHAT SONG DID YOU SING AT THAT PARTY IN
LONDON?

RUDY: Err, 'We Are the Champions'...

Sometimes, interviewers will ask the same question again and
again at unexpected times, to try to catch their interviewee
fibbing. When they realize they've made one mistake, some
liars will begin to fall apart and eventually start to tell the truth.

But there are other, less pleasant, techniques that have been used by secret service 'interrogators'.

Some are designed to completely confuse the suspect and make them crack. For instance:

- *Keeping the subject in the dark*
- *Interviewing them for eighteen hours a day, day after day, week after week*
- *Not allowing them food*
- *Making the room very hot – or very cold*
- *Stopping them from sleeping*

One other method of creating confusion is to bombard your target with ridiculous babble, until they can stand no more (this might sound crazy, but secret services have used it). So you might leave Rudy in his interrogation cell, and, through a loudspeaker, blast him with:

> 'CABBAGES ARE YELLOW, BORN IN THE MORNING, THEY
> MOVE LIKE LAMBS. NOT THERE — YOU SAID TREE?'

Complete and utter nonsense!

Try making up your own babble and try it on a friend – and see how long they last before they'll do anything for you to be quiet and leave them alone! *(Might be a good one to try on your mum when she won't get out of your room.)*

Or an interrogator might come up with a faked confession by someone else known to be involved in the secret plots.

You might pretend that you've already captured General Pedro and this is what he had to say:

> 'It was all Rudy. He planned everything.
> He made me do it! I am an innocent victim!
> That worm Rawcus is the bad guy here.
> Signed, General Pedro.'

Show this to Rudy and he might decide it's better for him to start to tell the truth – after all, he doesn't want to take more of the blame than he deserves. Or he might realize that this is just the kind of technique you're likely to use – and keep his mouth shut. What then?

You could always try the good cop/ bad cop routine. You'll have seen versions of this on TV. Your colleague Will could play the part of the bad cop, while you'll be the goodie. This is how your interview with Rudy might go:

```
TRANSCRIPT OF INTERVIEW WITH 'RUDY' RAWCUS.
1 OCTOBER. 04.00.

YOU: OK, Rudy, we've been here a while. It really
will be better for you if you just tell me what
you've been up to. That way I can protect you.
I can keep your punishment down.

WILL: TELL ME NOW, YOU TWO-TIMING SPYING
TRAITOR, OR YOU'LL REGRET IT.

YOU: You heard him, Rudy. I can't control him.
Tell me everything.
```

WILL: YOU'VE GOT FIVE SECONDS OR I'LL BE
BACK WITH THE ELECTRIC SHOCK KIT - AND YOU
WON'T BE LOOKING PRETTY.

YOU: Last chance, Rudy. I can save you. I trained
with you. I know you. Believe me.

WILL: FIVE ... FOUR ...

RUDY: OK! OK! I'll tell you everything. Just keep
that crazy guy away from me!

Just because you've seen it on TV doesn't mean it's fiction.
The good cop/bad cop routine is used by intelligence
organizations all around the world.

So what if you try it on Rudy – and it works?

Then, you've done it! You've got a confession – he really
was working with Pedro and his contact in China on
Operation Esmeralda – a project to provide arms to
dangerous terrorists. Your spy psychology has served you
well. It's been a job well done.

But psychology isn't only important when you need to make
a target talk. You'll also need knowledge about how people's
minds work to recruit your own agents. And some spy
agencies have looked at using the mind for stupendously
strange **psychic operations**. Read on to find out more ...

KNOW YOUR RECRUIT

You're in Pakistan, on a special SIS mission to recruit a weapons scientist who works in a top government lab. You want him or her to betray their own country by passing on secrets to you. How could you possibly make them do it?

Firstly, you have to identify some likely candidates. Let's say you're undercover as a military attaché at the embassy. That will give you plenty of opportunity to meet scientists working in the weapons business. You soon learn that there's one scientist who loves his country, and who's having an affair that his wife doesn't know about. A second loves England and goes there on holiday whenever he can. A third is upset with her job because she thinks she's badly paid.

And already you have three ways in:

1. **Blackmail:** You tell the first scientist that you'll reveal the truth about his affair – unless he agrees to forward one or two little titbits of information to you.
2. **Temptation:** You tell the second that you can arrange a permanent work visa and a transfer to England for the scientist and his family – if only he can offer you a little help in return.
3. **Money:** You offer cash for secrets.

Getting to know your targets in advance is vital. For example, offering money to scientist number one might well get you nowhere – he might even tell his own authorities about you because someone who loves his country is likely to need a better incentive than some cash to betray it.

But if this might sound like quite straightforward psychology, there's another sort that definitely is not.

Which of the following do you think is a real programme that has actually been run by an intelligence agency?

1. STARBURST – the use of psychics (people who claim to have extraordinary mental abilities) to explode people or objects in another room or country.

2. STARGATE – the use of psychics to 'see' events or people or objects in another room, another building – or another country.

3. STARBURN – the use of psychics to penetrate people's minds and check whether they're loyal agents – or traitors.

Answer:
2. Project Stargate was a real programme run by the CIA. So-called 'remote viewers' were recruited and trained. These people could supposedly 'see' events from huge distances away. Their job was to provide intelligence.

For example, according to one report, a remote viewer 'saw' that a KGB colonel was smuggling information using a communications device hidden in a pocket calculator. When intelligence officers later captured the colonel they told him they knew about the calculator – and he decided that they knew so much, he'd better cooperate.

The CIA started work with remote viewers in the 1970s, and reportedly used them right through to the mid 1990s. But in the end they decided that, when properly evaluated, the programme had not been useful to them.

But if psychics haven't been a great help to intelligence agencies, there are other 'tools' that are invaluable. You already know about communications gadgets and surveillance devices. But that's only the start.

You've got Rudy's confession. But now you need to get rid of the threat from General Pedro. Just what would you need for a night-time sabotage mission to his remote base? Turn the page to find out . . .

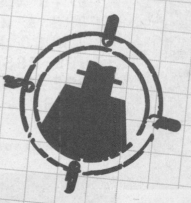

CHAPTER 6

ESSENTIAL KIT

CLASSIFIED

JUST AS JAMES BOND
GOES TO VISIT 'Q'
BEFORE A MISSION, YOU
WILL ALSO NEED TO
GATHER ESSENTIAL KIT
BEFORE YOU SET OFF ON
PEDRO'S TAIL.

So where will *you* go?

TOP SECRET

NAME: OFFICE OF TECHNICAL SERVICE (OTS), CIA

PURPOSE: Technical support to CIA officers working in the field - including the provision of weapons and gadgets

OTS specialists are based with CIA stations around the world.

The UK's SIS is more secretive about its gadget-makers – but it has them too, of course.

The real-life inspiration for 'Q' was a man called Charles Fraser-Smith.

SPY SUPREMO

Name: CHARLES FRASER-SMITH
Lived: 1904–1992

Fraser-Smith was a brilliant inventor who created ingenious gadgets for the SIS and for earlier intelligence agencies during the Second World War. Some of his real-life hits include:

· Maps printed in invisible ink on

> handkerchiefs. (The maps appeared
> when you soaked them in urine!)
> · Cigarette lighters containing mini-
>   cameras
> · Edible notepaper (based on rice
>   paper)
> · Chess pieces containing secret
>   compartments
> · Buttons concealing a compass

Your mission is this: to penetrate the base of General Pedro, search for useful info, sabotage any vital equipment and get out fast.

To accomplish this, you're going to need the latest high-tech gadgets.

Let's start with what you'll wear.

ACTION GEAR

Your clothes will have to be as tough as you are. They'll need to keep you safe from a knife-wielding assassin – or, worse, a bullet.

So what if you're on a mission and someone's firing at you? Well, you run. If you can't? You hope your body armour will do the trick.

Spencer Bing is a man on a mission of his own: to work out how that armour actually works . . .

TIME: Early
PLACE: Field in the middle of
nowhere
STATE OF MIND: Upset

I'm standing at the end of a field and
there's a man pointing a gun at me.

TRANSLATION: I'm in deep trouble

It's cold, it's boggy and, even worse,
I'm dressed only in a pair of underpants and
a 'bulletproof vest'.

Right. He's picking up the gun. (Gulp.)
He's taking aim . . .

. . . THUMP

Bing's on his back . . . but that vest stopped the bullet going into his body. **How did it do it?**

First, picture yourself on the football pitch, kicking a monumental goal. You smash it into the back of the net and the goalposts wobble! When a bullet hits an armour vest, the layers of that vest slow the bullet right down and flatten its point, stopping it from reaching your flesh. Body armour is often made from Kevlar – a very tough, but very light-weight material. But the impact can still cause bruises.

Of course, to be totally effective, your body armour will have to protect you against a wide range of weapons, some stranger than others. In fact, you might not even know when you're under attack . . . Peak inside the velvet-lined cabinet that holds Sir Stephen's collection and you'll be amazed. Each and every one of these devices was really invented for use by a spy:

I. THE COBRA-VENOM GUN

The cobra may be a crafty killer, but this dart was made by a being with even more cunning – a scientist with the CIA. The tip of this dart is sharp, but it will do no more than sting the skin. No, the danger lies in the coating of the tip, which consists of that snake's deadly venom! Use the gun in England and doctors examining the target's blood will know that something strange has been afoot. But use it in a country where cobras live, like India – and doctors will believe the victim was simply bitten by a snake in a tragic accident . . .

2. THE CIGARETTE PISTOL

Imagine a tiny gun the exact size and shape of a cigarette – and much more deadly. Around the metal barrel is a coating, designed to make it look like the real thing. But attached to the end that goes into your mouth is a little string . . . Pull on it with your teeth and a single bullet will be blasted out the other end! A devilish invention. But one that didn't go far because, to take out an enemy, one had to lean close – the bullet could travel only about a metre from the mouth.

3. THE KILLER UMBRELLA

Few would look at the humble umbrella and think 'deadly weapon'. But then few have my experience in the field ... It was the KGB – spy agency of the former Soviet Union, and employer of many of my greatest adversaries – that developed an umbrella with a minute poison pellet in its tip.

A Bulgarian journalist was killed using this technique in 1978. As he was standing on a bridge in London, the special umbrella was jabbed at his leg. The poison was fired into his thigh – and he died soon afterwards.

4. THE BOTTOM GUN

You need a hiding place for a gun – somewhere it's unlikely to be found. Your pocket? Too obvious. In your belt? Far too risky. Up your bottom? Well, yes ... this is another uncomfortable invention of the KGB. The tiny, tube-like pistol was kept in a rubber container and could be securely hidden until it was required. Thankfully, I, Sir Stephen, was never required to resort to concealing a weapon in such a cavity ...

5. THE GAS PEN

Imagine a pen that contains not ink, but gas. Tear gas, in fact – which is still used by police today to quell rioting crowds. Unpleasant stuff. When it hits your eyes, it makes them sting and water. British inventors created the pen, which fires gas from a nozzle in the end, to help British agents during the Second World War.

Now back to preparations for your current mission. You've got the bulletproof kit. But what else might you wear that would help with the job?

Well, for your approach to the general area of the base, you might consider a jacket with solar panels. These panels provide electricity to power your gadgets, so you can save your batteries for later.

But to increase your chances of sneaking up close to the base without being spotted, you should wait until night. In fact, many spy missions are conducted under the cover of darkness. And you'll need the kit to suit.

Although it will be dark, you'll still need to consider disguise. You won't need the full works – but you will need to use camouflage. Choosing dark-coloured clothes to blend into the night-time background is Day One Spy School stuff. But you could also smear your rucksack, shoes and equipment with a high-tech camouflage gel.

FISHY BUSINESS

The gel has been developed by British scientists – and it's based on the amazing colour-changing capabilities of the cuttlefish. This sea creature can match any background and do it lightning-fast. How? As well as changing the pigments in its body, certain cells in its skin also act a bit like a mirror. They reflect back the main colours of light surrounding it, helping it to blend in. The scientists have made a gel that works in a similar way to these cells – perfect for soldiers and spies!

In fact, animals have been the inspiration for a whole range of gadgets and products that you could use on missions.

Spencer Bing spent three months visiting labs around the world and compiling a special report. Here are just a few of the highlights:

1. LOCATION: Portland, United States
ANIMAL INSPIRATION: Gecko
PRODUCT: Super-super-stickiness!

Geckos can scamper up and down glass walls with ease, and hold on with only a single toe . . . A closer look at their bodies revealed that tiny hairs on their toes provide their amazing sticking power. American scientists have copied the little-hair technique, and reckon it could be used for really advanced non-slip gloves and climbing equipment.

2. LOCATION: Boston, USA
ANIMAL INSPIRATION: Scorpion
PRODUCT: Robo-scorpion!

This mini-robot is modelled on a scorpion. It's solar-powered and can travel deep into a desert, gathering data all the time. If you needed to survey a remote desert camp, you could send in Robo-scorpion first for a bit of reconnaissance!

It would be nice, of course, if you could borrow other animal *strengths*. What if you had muscles like a chimpanzee and you could plan on swinging yourself to General Pedro's base at high speed?

Imagine this: over your camouflage kit you strap a suit of muscles. You even slot artificial muscles in your shoes – and as you run, they become energized, helping you leap over a high wall with ease!

In fact, scientists all around the world are right now working on just this sort of body-boosting kit. The artificial muscles are mostly made from certain types of plastic – though some are even made from the building blocks of real animal muscle.

But extra energy is little use to you if you can't actually see the wall you need to jump over. Of course you can't run around the base with a torch – if you did, you'd be seen and captured in seconds. So how will you see in the dark? The answer is:

NIGHT-VISION GOGGLES

There are two different approaches to improving your vision at night:

1. Light-boosting: These systems collect every last little bit of light available – including light that your own eyes can't even see. Then they artificially boost it, so that you can make out an image. You can think of this system as giving you the vision of an animal with excellent night-sight, like a cat.

2. Heat-imaging: This approach isn't based on light, but on infrared energy given out by objects (including people) as heat. Using this technique, you'll quickly be able to spot a person hiding in a forest. The reddish-orange outline of the warm person will give them away. This type of goggle set-up will help you spot the general's guards way before they see you.

But being able to see your way won't necessarily mean you'll find it easy to locate the base. You may need to use some navigational aids.

SATELLITE SUPPORT
There are at least twenty-four 'Global Positioning System' (GPS) satellites in orbit around the Earth at any one time. And these satellites constantly emit signals. Your GPS receiver will use these signals to calculate its distance from four separate satellites. Using this information, it will work out your exact position on the surface of the Earth to within one metre. Your handset will then display your position on a map.

But what if your GPS unit fails? If you know that you need to go south-west to get to the base, you could use an:

ELECTRONIC COMPASS

Compasses use the Earth's magnetic field to determine the position of the North Pole. You can then use this information to keep a course along any direction you like. Electronic compasses simply display your direction and the usual North-South-East-West (and in between) points of a compass on a screen – making them easy to use.

BUILDING RECOGNITION

Scientists at Cambridge University in England are creating a very smart system for spies that get lost. You'll use your mobile phone to take a snap of your surroundings, then you'll send that picture to a remote computer. The computer will compare it with images in a database – and tell you where you are. The only downside is that, at the moment, the system can only help you if you're lost in Cambridge city centre . . .

So, now you've got the kit you'll need to get to the base. But what will you need when you get close?

You'll have to slink your way around the building to find a way in. As you do it, wouldn't it be nice to be able to see if there's anyone on the other side of the wall in a room that you're about to burst into?

Sounds crazy?

In fact, 'through-the-wall' research is hot stuff with the United States military. Their scientists have developed a device that you wear on your arm and that uses very low-power radar to detect someone moving around behind brick. Other similar technologies will let you spot if that moving person is carrying a weapon.

Use this kit and you can check through a closed doorway that there are no guards in the room inside, and you can make your way into the base unnoticed.

Now you need to think about what kit you'll need for when you're inside.

Your first mission is to collect information. So you'll need to take pictures of everything you see, including any maps or diagrams left lying around. For this, you'll need a **mini digital camera** – the sort you could conceal in your palm or disguise as another piece of equipment.

Then you might need somewhere to hide that camera, with its vital evidence. If you don't and you're captured, it'll be quickly found and taken from you. And, if you escape, the mission will be a waste of time if you make it out of the base, but your pictures don't.

So where will you put it?

In fact, good methods of concealing gadgets can be as important as the gadgets themselves.

One popular spot for concealment has always been the heel of a shoe. And historically, heel spaces were used by spies for carrying film. So if your camera is not disguised as something innocent, like a pen, you might want to ask for a pair of shoes with hidden compartments.

Now you're almost set. You've got the basic kit that you'll need to penetrate and investigate the base. All you need now is a way of getting there. And every top spy should travel in style . . .

CHAPTER 7

MOVE IT!

YOU NEED A MEANS OF
GETTING TO YOUR
MISSION DESTINATION -
AND BEYOND.

And you can forget boring old cars,
trains and passenger aircraft. Spies
have much more exciting options!

But before you decide exactly what you'll need to get to Pedro's base, let's cover all possible spying eventualities. Because every top operative needs to know how to get around on land, under water and in the air.

LAND!

You need a road-going vehicle. What would you choose?

- *A rusty bicycle?*
- *A police car?*
- *A surveillance van?*
- *None of the above?*

Well, at the very least, you'll want a car with bulletproof glass and armoured components. But how about a laser gun – or electrified handles?

If you want them, they're yours. In fact, the US Army Automotive Research Center has just the thing. The SmarTruck looks a bit like a regular off-road vehicle, but, as well as the gun and the special handles, you can also opt for:

- **Night-vision cameras**
- **Tear-gas-canister launchers**
- **A laser-guided missile launcher** (and a missile system that will intercept and destroy missiles fired at you!)
- A module containing a **tiny remote-control aircraft** –

you can send it off to collect video, which it then transmits live back to the truck

- Chemical and biological **weapons sensors**
- **A computer system** that will intercept emails or phone calls for you – or send fake emails to your enemy
- **Infrared headlights** for discreet night-time travelling. These headlights can also be used to transmit Morse-code messages (sequences of short and long signals, each encoding letters of the alphabet) between SmarTrucks in a convoy. Brush up on your Morse and you could even have a chat while in transit

SIR STEPHEN'S TOP TIP:

Here's how to say: 'Pull over, I am hungry' in Morse code.

.__. .._ ._.. ._.. / ___ ..._ . ._. /
.. / ._ __ / ... .._ _. __ ._. _._ /

Each dot stands for a short burst, and each dash for a long burst. You can use bursts of noise – or, in this case, bursts of infrared light.

Body armour and bulletproof glass come as standard on the SmarTruck, of course. The people who designed the truck say it can withstand a .44 magnum handgun fired at close range.

But how does the glass do it?

Like Kevlar, it absorbs the impact of the bullet, stopping it bursting through. Standard bulletproof glass is made up of a glass sandwich, with a layer of tough, see-through plastic in between. An incoming bullet would pierce that outer layer of glass, but be stopped by the plastic filling.

While the SmarTruck is perfect for when it doesn't matter if someone notices you, forget it if you're trying to travel incognito. All that gadgetry means that in a line-up of cars on the highway, yours would be easily picked out as the spy-mobile. And all the unwanted attention could drive you round the bend!

For days when you feel you need to keep your cover, you might choose to use a custom-made 'regular' car. You can order these cars over the internet. This is how an ad might read:

Warning: *if your mum borrows the car, tell her not to touch any of those extra controls . . .*

OK, that's not bad. But what if you're being chased, and your in-car GPS system shows you there's a lake dead ahead? If you're in an 'amphibious vehicle', you could escape your pursuers by going truly off-road . . .

LAND AND WATER!

'Amphibious' simply means able to operate on land or in water. A frog is amphibious. And so are some vehicles. To change from land to water mode you will need to:

- Switch steering from the wheels to a rudder (though sometimes the front wheels can be used as rudders in the water)
- Switch power from the wheels to a propeller

You might have seen pictures of hefty amphibious army vehicles on TV. But choosing a land/water vehicle doesn't mean you have to sacrifice elegance and speed. In fact, there's an amphibious sports car on the market that can do 200 kilometres per hour on land – and 80 kilometres per hour on water. The car uses a hydrofoil – a wing-like structure – to lift it up and slightly out of the water, so it skims along the surface.

SIR STEPHEN'S TOP TIP . . .
. . . *for avoiding a sinking feeling*

If you've been shot at, make sure there are no bullet holes in your amphibious vehicle before attempting to enter the lake!

WATER!

An amphibious vehicle could be perfect for making an unexpected escape – or crossing a bay, when you know you'll have a long drive ahead. But what if you were busy making contacts at an embassy party and these orders came through:

> TO: OUR TOP AGENT
> FROM: HQ
> INTERNATIONAL TERRORIST MASTERMIND CODENAME
> PMY SPOTTED ARRIVING BY HELICOPTER AT HIS
> MALDIVES RETREAT. PURSUE AND OBSERVE.

So you need to sneak up on an island – and you need to do it without being spotted. But how?

Spencer Bing has been researching your options. And he's whittled them down to two.

1. SCUBA DIVING
   To be a SCUBA (Self-Contained Underwater Breathing Apparatus) star, you will need:

· **Face mask (so you can see properly)**
· **Flippers (so you can move about with ease)**
· **Wetsuit or drysuit (to keep you warm)**
· **Buoyancy vest and weights (to control your depth)**
· **Cylinders containing compressed air (so you can breathe)**
· **Mouthpiece (to deliver that vital air!)**

Notes: If you're wearing a wetsuit, you will get wet. But if the suit fits properly, it will trap a layer of water over your skin. Your body heat will soon warm up this layer, and you'll be able to keep going without shivering for much longer than if you were wearing your regular swimming-pool kit.

A drysuit really does keep you dry, so it's perfect for even colder conditions.

To keep yourself extra snug, you could wear a fleecy layer underneath.

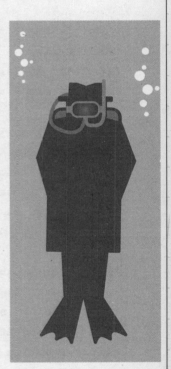

BING'S VERDICT:

Pluses:
· Effective — you can stay underwater for hours
· Easy to use — once you've been trained

Minuses:
· You're under your own power — and if you run out of swimming energy, you're seriously stuck
· Bulky to carry around — no way could you turn up at a cocktail party with your SCUBA kit hidden in your jacket pocket
· When you breathe out, that air forms bubbles in the water, which then rise to the surface.

A keen-eyed defender of an evil mastermind's island hideaway could spot those bubbles — and your mission (and you) could be over

But let's look at that last minus first. Because there is a way to overcome it ...

TIME: Early
LOCATION: Indian Ocean
STATE OF MIND: Nervous

I'm sitting on the edge of a speedboat, about to tip myself back into shark-infested waters. On my feet, huge flippers. On my back, a huge air cylinder. In my hand, my 're-breathing' mouthpiece.

My friendly instructor tells me that when I breathe out, that air won't be released to form noisy bubbles in the sea. Instead, it will feed back into the SCUBA cylinder system. With some clever tweaking (automatic — or so he says), there'll still be enough oxygen coming through to keep me alive. Here goes . . .

HALF AN HOUR LATER: It works! I'm bubble-free — and alive!

So that's the bubbles dealt with. How about the problem of bulk?

Well, there is a possible solution. You could always use a **mini-breather**.

The smallest practical mini-breather available today wouldn't fit easily in your jacket pocket at the embassy party – but you could keep it in a briefcase. In place of the full SCUBA kit, you get an air cylinder about the same size as a fizzy drinks can, and a mouthpiece.

But there is a downside. With a cylinder this size, you'll only get enough air for about forty breaths. That translates into only a few minutes of underwater swimming time ...

Now to the first minus of SCUBA diving to the island: you have to do all the work. Instead of swimming underwater, you might consider using something that comes with its own power. And this is Bing's second suggestion for a method across.

2. **Personal Submarine**
   There are a number of mini-subs to choose from.

   A version that might fit the bill is a one-person sub that can keep going for up to eight hours at a time and travel at a speed of six knots (that's about eleven kilometres per hour — or about twice walking speed).

BING'S VERDICT:

Pluses:
- Next-to-no effort on your part
- You keep dry
- Sharks will find it harder to bite through the sub than a wetsuit

Minuses:
- Not exactly super-speedy
- Bulky. And you have to somehow transport it to the water You'll probably need at least a pick-up truck to do this — and someone could spot you

So, SCUBA diving and a personal sub are two possibilities for making it across to the island. But what if the orders had read:

INTERNATIONAL TERRORIST MASTERMIND CODENAME PMY SPOTTED ARRIVING BY HELICOPTER AT HIS MALDIVES RETREAT. PURSUE AND OBSERVE. IMMEDIATELY.

If there's no time to gather your SCUBA kit or get the personal sub from its hiding spot, you might have to swim unaided. But there's no excuse for being unprepared. Because under your smart embassy party gear, you could be wearing **amphibious clothes**.

Spencer Bing went to a special fashion show to check them out.

TIME: Late
LOCATION: New York

I'm in a warehouse, inspecting the
latest in United States Navy SEAL
(that's the elite SEa-Air-Land special forces
group) clothing technology. On the catwalk is
Steve. And he's wearing a diving suit that you
can ALSO wear out of the water. This is what
Steve told me:

'Divers who wear normal drysuits have to change
out of them when they reach land. If they
didn't, they'd get far too hot. But this means
they have to carry dry clothes with them. If
you choose this new suit, you can wear it in
the water and then out of it — it's perfect for
both. How?

'The answer lies in its three layers.

'Layer one, closest to the skin: an insulating
layer that reflects body heat and keeps you
warm in the water. Layer two: a plastic layer.
Layer three, the outer layer: a stretchy
fabric, designed so you'll slip easily through
the water.

'It's the special plastic layer that's really
important. The plastic behaves differently

depending on the temperature. At fairly low
temperatures — the kind you'll experience
during an ocean swim — it stops water from
passing through, so keeps you warm and dry.
At higher temperatures — the kind you'll
experience when you're walking around on
land — it lets sweat out, so you don't overheat.'

So, now you know your options for travelling on land or
in water — or both. But you also need to know how to get
about in . . .

AIR!

Which of the following do you think could be real options?

1. *A personal jetpack*
2. *A fold-up plane*
3. *Teleportation (press a button and you'll vanish and
   reappear at your chosen destination)*

Answer:

1. Personal jetpacks certainly exist. For instance, one
   stuntman recently got to forty-three metres — the height
   of a twelve-storey building — using a jetpack. But they're
   not quite ready for general use. Keeping them safe and
   stable when they're high in the air isn't easy.
2. Well, there are planes that have folding wings.
   Aeroplanes stored on aircraft carriers, for use by navy
   pilots, fold their wings to save space. But that's about as

compact as you can get.

3. Scientists are trying to work out ways to instantly transport matter through space – but this work is at a very, very early stage. At the moment, if you want to travel through the air, you'll need a craft to carry you.

But you won't always use aircraft to pick you up and drop you off at your destination. Sometimes you'll use them to drop you out of the sky!

Learning to parachute is an important part of your spy training. First, you'll do it during the day. Then at night. All parachuting involves jumping out of an aircraft and letting loose your canopy. But there are a few different approaches.

TIME: 02.00 hours
LOCATION: No idea
STATE OF MIND: Terrified

I'm in the cargo hold of a giant plane and the DOOR IS OPEN! There's a man in a beret and camouflage gear and he WANTS ME TO JUMP OUT. I've got this parachute strapped to my back and he's yelling at me . . .

INSTRUCTOR: Hey, you, get up! We're going for a heigh-ho.

ME: What?

INSTRUCTOR: I said: get up and make it fast!
You're going to miss the target!

ME: A heigh-ho?

INSTRUCTOR (really shouting now): NOW, BING,
NOW!

In fact, the 'heigh-ho' – really the HAHO – is just one style of jump. There are a number of them, but learn these two terms and you'll impress your spy school buddies:

1. HALO This stands for High-Altitude, Low-Opening. You'll be dropped from a great height and you'll spend a few minutes in free fall before you finally open your canopy. This will give you a fast descent to your target on the ground.

2. HAHO High-Altitude, High-Opening. You'll be dropped from a great height, but you'll open your canopy very soon afterwards. This means you'll have a long journey down to the ground. But it also means that the aircraft that drops you off can stay well away from your target spot – so it's less likely to be noticed. You'll use hand controls to steer yourself to the right location.

Got all that? Good. Then you know the basics. But there are other, stranger transport options that you might want to keep in mind for just the right occasion. How about:

ICE MAGIC

You need to traverse an icy expanse. You could perhaps use skis or a dog sled – or you could go for the Ice Bike. Created by an American inventor, it has no plastic parts which could get so cold they shatter. But it does have huge tyres for a good grip on a slippery surface. Trial rides in Antarctica showed it works well even in the toughest conditions.

SUPER SURFING

A jet-powered surfboard could be just the thing for a mission in a beach-side location. Get a tan and bleach your hair and you could go undercover as a surfer. A small engine attached to the board will help you whizz across the ocean, making it perfect for powering out to catch some early morning waves – as well as for trailing targets at sea!

BIKE-BOAT

This is a bike that you can convert to a boat in minutes. You carry two inflatable floats, a propeller and rudder in a backpack while you're cycling. Then, if you find an inconvenient canal in your way, you assemble the floats and control system, plonk the bike on top and you can 'cycle' along the water.

SLIDE TO SAFETY

You're based in a flash apartment building in the centre of New York. You're on the eleventh floor – and you see, from your window, a gang you've been trailing burst through the front door, bristling with weapons. They're on their way up in the lift and on the stairs. There are too many of them for you to take on. You need to get out. But how? It's far too far to jump . . . But you could use a safety chute. The chute looks a bit like a slide you'd slip down in a water park. But it's made from Kevlar (the tough material used for bulletproof clothes), and it's packed in a space in the outer wall of your building. All you need to do is press a button to spring it open. It will uncoil, you'll leap into it and you'll be safely on the ground in less than twenty seconds!

OK, now you're ready to make your selection for the trip to Pedro's base. What would you go for?

In this case, a good option might be to pack up all your kit and organize a HAHO parachute jump. Then, using your satellite navigation system, you can trek cross-country direct to the base.

Once you get there, you know what to do.

Let's say you're successful. You make it inside, you take pictures of everything you see, you copy Pedro's computer hard drives and on the way out you plant explosives to blow up the base.

You escape unharmed and you trek back to the pick-up

point, where a helicopter is waiting to evacuate you to safety.

The mission was a success. You have lists of Pedro's contacts; you know how far the arms deals had gone. Your boss congratulates you . . .

Think the Rudy–Pedro case is closed?

Think again.

But first, there's some final spy preparation in store. **Turn to Chapter 8 to find out more.**

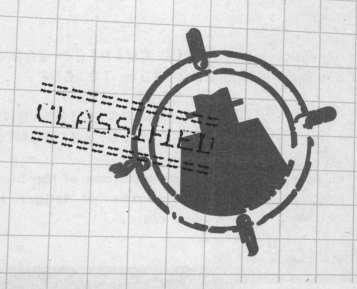

CHAPTER 8

NEED TO KNOW

CLASSIFIED

IN THIS CHAPTER YOU'LL
LEARN HOW TO COPE
WITH SOME LIFE-
THREATENING SCENARIOS
SPIES COULD ENCOUNTER.

**We'll start with one of the biggest
potential sources of danger. Here
are some clues:**

- **They have no hands**
- **They won't listen to reason**
- **They can't speak**
- **They're inhuman!**

In fact, they're animals.

The Memoirs of Sir Stephen
CHAPTER 458: BITE FRIGHT

It's a frosty winter's night and here I am, warm beside the fire, writing my memoirs, my faithful beagle's head upon my slipper. Her eyes are closed, her paws trembling as she dreams of running in the fields behind my mansion. What could be less of a threat than this little dog? And yet, I, Sir Stephen, know better than most what dastardly adversaries animals can be. When I think of that night in Sydney Harbour, handcuffed to a buoy, bobbing in the ocean, the sight of a fin zooming towards me . . . My hand shakes. My heart shivers. And yet I fought the shark and survived. But delay your congratulations, my dear reader. For fighting a shark was not the greatest animal challenge that I have had to meet. One dark night in Florida, I was thrown by an angry Polish agent into a pool of alligators. Dawn in Siberia, I faced a rabid wolf. Midnight in Dubai, a crazed camel came lurching towards me. Afternoon in rural Afghanistan . . . *(Editor's note: this goes on for some time.)*

Of course, you can't prepare for every animal eventuality. So here are Sir Stephen's top tips for dealing with the dangerous beasts that you're most likely to encounter on some of your more exotic missions.

SIR STEPHEN'S TOP TIPS:

I. ALLIGATORS

Covering an alligator's eyes should calm it down – as well as making it trickier for it to attack. So take off your shirt and throw it over the creature's head. Then try to roll the alligator over and push down as hard as you can on its neck. This should prevent it from clamping one of your limbs in its jaws. Then . . . call for help!

2. SNAKES

It's not obvious which snakes are poisonous and which are not, so take no chances. But while some (like the king cobra) will happily attack, most will slither away as soon as they sense you. To reduce your risk of a bite in snake country, look very carefully where you're walking. And if you do kill a snake for an emergency supper, chop off its head before you go anywhere near those fangs. Because for a short time afterwards, even a dead snake can still bite!

3. BEARS

If a bear charges at you because you've come too close to it or its cubs, stand your ground. Often, the bear will stop short of you. If it doesn't, drop to the earth, with your face down, and keep still. What happens next is very important, and will determine your ultimate response. If the bear doesn't try to eat you, stay still until it realizes you're not a threat and it has moved right away. But if it does start to eat you, fight back as viciously as you can!

4. SHARKS

The only way to survive a shark attack is to hope the shark loses interest, or to fight your way out of it. Use your fists or your feet to hit a shark's eyes or its gills – these are the most sensitive spots. If you use enough force, many sharks will get scared and swim off.

But if you know you're likely to be swimming in shark-infested waters, you might consider coming prepared with an 'anti-shark' device. This gadget attaches to your body and produces an electric field, which you won't feel, but which will cause a shark severe pain if it comes too close. A lightweight chain-mail suit could be an alternative. If a shark closes its jaws around your arm, the chain-mail should stop those teeth slicing straight through your flesh.

There is one other option for incapacitating a shark. It won't work in the open ocean. But if your enemy is the sort who likes to keep sharp-toothed pets in his own swimming pool – and he thinks you'd just love a 'relaxing' swim – you might want to reach for the **Liquid Nightmare**.

This is a chemical reportedly created for the CIA. It comes in a little bottle and, when you add it to water, it quickly converts that water into a gel. So if you move fast enough, you just might be able to trap the shark before it reaches you – and put it in a sticky situation all of its own!

Now you're better prepared to deal with animal attacks. But what about the human sort? And what if you've been overwhelmed and you're captured or hurt – and you need to escape?

Imagine this:

```
FROM: HQ

TO: OUR TOP AGENT

FURTHER    PEDRO-RELATED    ACTIVITY.    GO
IMMEDIATELY   TO   NORTHERN   NORWAY.   LOCATE
SECRET   LAIR   OF   PEDRO'S   CHINESE   CONTACT.
INFILTRATE AND REPORT.
```

So you get to northern Norway. You find the holiday home of the Chinese contact.

But it's a trap. Those orders weren't from HQ at all – they were from some of the angry survivors of your attack on Pedro's base! As you approach the house, you're bitten by a guard dog and you're captured. You're thrown into a truck and you're taken on an hour-long journey, then tied up in an underground cell . . .

What do you do?

Spencer Bing has been doing his research.

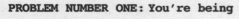

ESCAPOLOGY: SECRET DOSSIER

PROBLEM NUMBER ONE: You're being
    tied up
SOLUTION: Push against those ropes as hard as you
    can. This will give you more room to
    manoeuvre later, to help work yourself free

PROBLEM NUMBER TWO: The guard dog has left a huge
    gash in your arm!
SOLUTION: Don't ignore the wound — you could lose
    so much blood that you'll faint

A spy heading out on a mission can call on science and technology officers for the very latest high-tech medical kit. If you're lucky, you'll still have it with you. These are some of the things it might contain:

SPY FIELD MEDICAL KIT

The chitosan bandage: *This dressing, based on the make-up of the shell of a prawn, can seal a major wound in an artery in minutes – stopping a wounded agent dying from a loss of gushing blood.*

Shape-shifting trouser linings: *Made from a fabric that can stiffen to form a splint around a broken bone.*

Hand-held ultrasound: *Uses blasts of sound to identify internal bleeding in an injured officer.*

So, if you have a chitosan bandage to hand, you can wrap it around your wound to stop the bleeding.

If you don't, take off a sock and tie it above the wound. Then hold your arm above your head. This will reduce the amount of blood that's pumped to it – and out of the hole!

PROBLEM NUMBER THREE: At last, you manage to
    escape from your underground cell. Your
    captors haven't spotted this — yet. And your
    plan is to get as far away as possible before
    they do. But you find yourself in freezing
    cold and deep snow — and night's approaching
SOLUTION: To stand any chance of surviving the
    night you need to get immediate shelter, out
    of the wind. Firstly work out which way the
    wind is blowing. Then dig a shelter in the
    snow, so that the wind will sweep past your
    entrance — not blast its way straight in

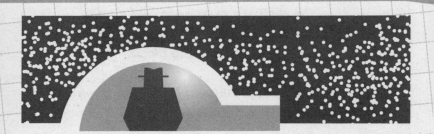

In the morning, you'll have to emerge from your shelter and seek help. To get that help, you'll need to communicate with your base . . . But what if Pedro's angry men have taken your watch, your phone, your GPS system, your personal tracking device – everything that you'd need to navigate your way to safety and get in touch with HQ? What do you do?

You were in the back of a truck when you were taken to your cell, so all you know is that you're an hour's drive from the house. You scan the horizon and recognize nothing. Now what? One good tip for finding civilization is to look for electricity pylons. Follow the wires and eventually you should find someone who can help you get in touch with your base.

But then, you'll need to be able to communicate.

TALKING TECH

There are hand-held translator gadgets available. These gadgets let you look up a word and discover its equivalent in the country you're in. The United States Defense Department has also created two advanced translation machines. With the first, called **Phraselator** you can speak a simple sentence in

English, and a computer-voice will read out a translation in one of two or three languages. The other device can translate documents into English from dozens of different languages!

But if your digital translator was taken from your pocket along with all your navigation and communication kit, you'll need to find another way of getting your message across. This will mean falling back on your **language training**.

You need to find a friendly local with a telephone, then you'll be able to call your boss and get help.

Here's how to say: 'Do you have a telephone?' in the following languages:

French *(also useful for Belgium, Switzerland, Lebanon, parts of Africa, Canada):*
Avez-vous un téléphone?
(AVAY-VOO URN TELEFON?)

Bengali *(use this in parts of India):*
Aapnaar ki telephone achhé?
(UP-NAAR KEE TELLY-FON ATCH-AY?)

Arabic *(the Middle East):*
Fi hatif?
(FEE HATEEF?)

Spanish *(also good for South America):*
¿Tiene usted un teléphono?
(TEE-YE-NAY OO-STED UN TELEFONO?)

Norwegian:
> **Har du en telefon?**
> (HAR DOO EN TELEFON?)

So, you find a house. And you ask for a telephone. The friendly couple invite you in, give you some food and let you sit by the fire. Thirty minutes pass, and a helicopter evacuation unit hovers above the snow outside. You thank the friendly couple, you strap yourself into the dangling harness and you're winched to safety.

In the helicopter are local intelligence agents and your boss. The house has been surrounded, he tells you. All Pedro's men have been captured. And the Chinese contact has been seized!

That's it. Your Rudy–Pedro–Chinese contact missions are over.

And so too is your training.

With the knowledge gained in these chapters, you've got all the info you'll need for life as a spy.

Now it's time for you to think about getting out there, taking a posting, and doing your job . . .

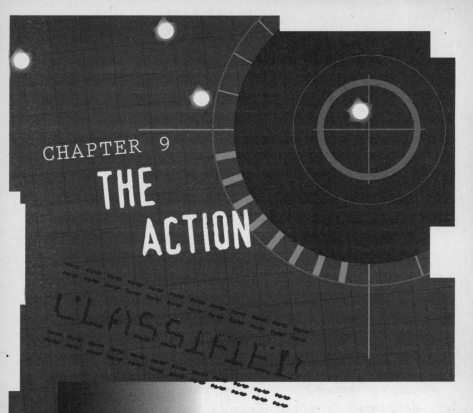

THE ACTION

CLASSIFIED

YOU'VE GOT THE KNOWLEDGE TO PREPARE YOU FOR LIFE AS A SPY.

But you should know that there's one more downside, apart from the risk to your life: you can't show off about it. While it could be OK to trust your family and a few very close friends with your secret, no one else must know. You'll have to work hard at describing 'boring' trips to 'dull' work meetings, or frequent holidays overseas.

'How was your trip?' someone will ask you.

This will be the truth: It was no holiday. You spent three weeks infiltrating a North African terrorist cell, one week withstanding torture in solitary confinement, two days when you believed each morning you might be eaten by a hungry Doberman . . . and three long nights dragging your starved, weary body (and planned dates of attacks on major embassies) to the nearest port and to safety.

This is what you'll say: 'Lovely, thanks. Very relaxing. Nice beach.'

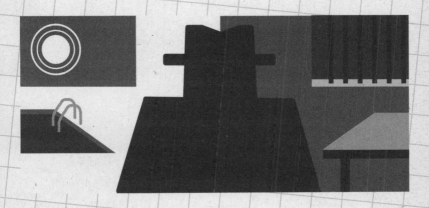

You'll get no public recognition for your service to your country. But you will get satisfaction from your work.

Of course, the exact type of work you'll do will change with shifts in world politics, society and technology. These days, there's lots of call for intelligence officers with really advanced computer skills – and also surveillance experts who can speak certain languages, such as Arabic.

When MI5 advertised for about a thousand new staff in 2004 (increasing its number of employees by one half!) it wanted:

- Surveillance experts
- People to thoroughly check out new recruits
- People who could speak Arabic, Urdu, Iranian, Turkish, Punjabi and Russian

These new staff are all based in the UK.

But, after the 11 September 2001 attacks in the USA, there has also been a new boom in the numbers of active foreign field agents who work on the ground abroad, talking to people and gathering vital information.

So if you do become a field officer, where might you go?

Right now, the Middle East and the Persian Gulf are major centres of action. You might take a post in Damascus, Syria . . . or even in Iraq.

If that doesn't put you off, you should start your preparation now. Learn another language, find out about other cultures and other countries. Work hard at school. Persuade your parents to take you on long holidays to far-flung destinations.

Because the more you learn about the world, and how to look after yourself and cope away from home, the more likely it is that you'll achieve your dream – and become a spy.

째애